ANNIE MAGDALENE

ANNIE MAGDALENE

A NOVEL

Barbara Hanrahan

BEAUFORT BOOKS
Publishers · New York

No character in this book is intended to represent any actual person; all the incidents of the story are entirely fictional in nature.

Library of Congress Cataloging-in-Publication Data

Hanrahan, Barbara.
Annie Magdalene.

I. Title.
PR9619.3.H3A8 1986   823   85-9164
ISBN 0-8253-0309-5

Published in the United States by Beaufort Books Publishers, New York.

Printed in the U.S.A.   First American Edition

10 9 8 7 6 5 4 3 2 1

For all the dinners are cooked; the plates and cups washed; the children sent to school and gone out into the world. Nothing remains of it all. All has vanished. No biography or history has a word to say about it. And the novels, without meaning to, inevitably lie . . . All these infinitely obscure lives remain to be recorded . . .

VIRGINIA WOOLF

Elderly working-class Australian woman recalls her life, her family, and her loves.

Granpa McGregor was having his dinner when the crystal chandelier fell down just behind his chair. It was an omen. Within a week he was dead and the bank went broke and Granma McGregor had to sell the Glasgow house and the country house and her carriages and Dad had to leave the college and follow big brother John, who was a bit of a devil, out to Capetown.

Mum knew Zulu because she was born in South Africa where there were lions in the hills and Granpa Duret had an ostrich farm. The monkeys came in dozens and Granma Duret put on a man's hat and pointed the gun at them, but she couldn't fire it, so the monkeys sat there and laughed. Mum had a pet monkey and she picked up the little ostrich feathers they didn't want for the capes and hats, tied them up and put them in a box and sold them back to Granpa.

Granma and Granpa Duret were French. Granma had been a doctor in Paris before she went to South Africa with Granpa. He was a man of money and bought up miles and miles of land. Granma had eleven children and looked after the black women when they had their babies. Before she died of appendicitis she made Mum promise to give up dancing.

First Dad drove trains; then he was in charge of the black men who worked in the diamond mines. When they knocked off they had to go into a room and undress and be searched. White men inspected the black men's

7

back passages because they shoved diamonds up there to get away with them. Some stuck diamonds up their noses, even swallowed them.

A woman Dad knew had a baby girl before she was married and gave it away to the black woman who did the housework. Dad rescued the baby and paid a Dutch nurse to look after her. She was six years old when my brother, Tom, was born and Dad brought her home. Mum named her Dorothy Alice, after Dad's first two initials back to front.

Doctors suggested a sea voyage to cure Dad's arthritis. A man in the steamer office told him to try Adelaide, Australia. An Irishwoman told Mum to take her advice and go with him – once they got away you couldn't trust them.

Tom had his second birthday as they struck a rough spot on the sea. Dorrie was a good shot at quoits and was called the demon bowler. Dad lost his hat over-board. Mum was terribly sick and ill, because she was a couple of months pregnant with me.

When they arrived in February 1908, it was a heat-wave. They stayed at the coffee palace next to the ice-skating rink and Mum wanted a pipe put through the wall to cool her bedroom. Every night when the other guests had gone to sleep, she sat in the bath with the shower dripping on her.

[2]

I was supposed to be called Anna Magdalene, the same as Mum, but Dad, being from Scotland, put Annie Magdalene on my birth certificate. In those days the men had to go and register their children and they made so many mistakes that people were getting called wrong names.

Old Dr Drummond brought me into the world at Mrs Turner's maternity home, where ladies were accommodated during accouchement – he was a kind doctor with light-coloured eyes. I was the delicate one of the family; Mum thought the tossing of the steamer on the way out from South Africa might have affected me.

We came home to a single-fronted house in the city, attached to two others. Our street went up a hill and our house was perched on top; you had to walk up five steps to get to the gate. There were snapdragons in the diamond-shaped beds on either side of the path, ferns along the edge of the verandah, and Mum grew her sunflowers by the fence.

A nurse came to look after me and one day when she was taking a bundle of clothes out to wash, my brother told her to kill it – he thought she had the baby. The first electric tram went down North Terrace at the end of our street and the nurse took me for a ride on it in her arms. I might have been the youngest baby to travel on the first tram.

9

I woke up on Christmas morning and a pink doll with fair curls and a mushroom-shaped hat was sitting on the chair. I saw her through the bars of my cot and shut my eyes quick because I thought she was a real person. Later I had a doll of hard celluloid, a baby doll with a rattle in its head, and you could take its clothes off and put it in the bath.

At daybreak, when everyone was still asleep, I'd go out to the back yard. We had a nectarine, a Satsuma plum, an apricot and a fig tree. The figs were flat and green, and a pale pink inside, but I couldn't eat too many of them, they worried me. I was always very free and easy to go to the lavatory but my brother was just the opposite. He had bowel trouble, and my mother had to go with him and press his bowels back inside again.

The lavatory was down the bottom of the yard. The fowl house was beside it and when the moon came up it shone right in – I saw the white fowls on their perch, gone to sleep.

We kept all the food in the cellar where it was cool, with shelves scrubbed clean and a window that let in plenty of light. Mum would sit there and crochet when it was hot.

We never went in for animal ornaments but we had some lovely vases. And there was a square plate, patterned over with tiny triangle things, that I called the convict dish (the pattern resembled the arrows on a convict's uniform, though it was really of tiny flowers).

Once when I was standing out the front I saw a big

shark going past on a horse trolley at the end of the street. I called out to Mum, but by the time she got there the head had gone past and she only saw the tail. It was the biggest shark ever caught and its skeleton was put in a long shed at the back of the Museum.

[3]

Dad had a first-class certificate for a still engine and a second-class certificate for a locomotive engine; he didn't drive trains any more, but looked after a boiler house in a factory. He was a bit of a dandy with a ginger moustache that he touched up with dye so it matched his black hair. He went to the tailor to have his suits made and never spilt things on his waistcoats because he wore a serviette tucked in his collar at dinner. He was a very fussy man with a box to put his hats in; even if he went out in the shed he never rolled his sleeves up. Mum said that when he went to bed he thought he was going to his wedding, because there he'd be in his pyjama suit, combing his hair straight. And he had special soft kid gloves, a walking-stick with a silver knob, a gold watch-chain and three or four watches that ticked in the bedroom all the time. Dad could whistle any tune that came into his mind, he came whistling out in the morning, bright as a new penny; Mum said she wished he wouldn't whistle, it got on her nerves. Dad smoked a pipe, a very small one – it must have the smallest bulb you could get, and he'd mix some white stuff up and line the pipe to make it smaller. The Temple Bar tobacco he smoked had a sweet smell; he never smoked in the house, only in the yard or the shed.

Mum was a lady, very quietly spoken, it was her great habit to call people 'dear'. She wore gold ear-rings with rubies and she had a ruby engagement ring with little diamonds. She had lovely white hands, and when she went to bed she'd read books in Dutch by candlelight so she didn't have to get out of bed to turn off the gaslight. If she sat down with her hair loose it touched the floor; her skirts came to the top of her shoes. She had a lot of plants with shiny leaves – she polished them with a soft rag till the leaves shone like silver. She liked stickjaw toffee and made strawberry tarts; she rubbed lotion on her arms against mosquitoes, she called caterpillars Hairy Pollies, she didn't like moths. She told me about the time when she was home with her sisters, but Lily died, and now no one wrote from South Africa (though once her girlfriend who was a milliner sent a parcel and there were pink bed-socks for Mum and an organdie hat for my doll, but I was past the stage of wanting dolls).

My sister, Dorrie, had a little nose that wriggled when she laughed and fair skin, black hair, greeny-grey eyes; she wasn't pretty, but she wasn't ugly either. Dorrie and I shared a bedroom. She was no sooner in bed than she was asleep; she'd just put her head on the pillow and off she'd go, and when she snored I'd sing out to her. She had a box to keep her secret things in (it had been Mum's linen box that came out from South Africa) and when she forgot to lock it I'd have a look in, but I didn't find anything much, just her handbags. We had a chest of drawers to keep our underwear in – I only had one drawer, Dorrie had two. I'd watch her put her bloomers on, and when she was fourteen she wore stays that laced across the back and did up with hooks and eyes down the front. She was a placid type of girl, a happy type – if you said to her, 'Go and sit over there,' she'd go; she wasn't my type at all. She tied her hair back with a big starched bow and went to work at Bottomley's shirt factory in Currie Street and came home with yarns about old Bottomley and the forelady. Dorrie made friends with Eileen, who worked at the biscuit factory, where she got free biscuits at Christmas and Easter, and they went boy-hunting on Sunday afternoons. Dorrie couldn't remember much about South Africa, but she often told the story about the dressmaker who always carried her good dressmaking scissors in her pocket and once when a black man exposed himself she cut it; but whether she cut it right off, Dorrie couldn't say.

My brother, Tom, had a cleft in his chin that he'd got from some ancestor and he was strong, you could see his muscles come up – he'd say, 'Feel that,' and I couldn't dent it. But he was scared of dogs, and he used to wander in his sleep and pick things up and drop them and Mum had to lead him back to bed. He didn't like meat so she just dished him up the vegetables; one day she bought him some fish but he wouldn't look at it. In his baby photo he had long fair curls and a dress with a tartan sash – I supposed it was to make him look like a girl so he wouldn't be grabbed for the slave traffic. He was a torment who wanted me to do everything he did; he'd go down to the railways and get covered in mud, and once he fell in the tar pit so Mum had to sit him in a dish of kerosene to loosen it off his bottom. When he dropped a piece of iron on his foot, it made a hole in his boot and a deep scar that he had all his life.

[4]

Mrs Rudd next door had cats and birds. She had a cockatoo that talked and green parrots and a galah. The cocky, Old Bill, didn't like men – if he saw a man he'd chase him; once he took a piece out of Dad's leg. When the old chap up the street walked past in his bowler hat, Old Bill sat out the front on the pagoda and put on an awful turn – swore at him, said 'You old bugger.' Old Bill could make a noise just as if he was pumping up a bike, and he could squeal like the brakes of a motor car, and count up to ten, and laugh in different voices. Mrs Rudd's daughter, Edna, wasn't a hundred per cent; she had a funny little laugh, and Old Bill used to laugh just like her. Mrs Rudd would put a board in front of him and tell him to write a letter and he'd scribble along with his beak and sign his name with a flourish. But when Old Bill went in his cage at night, and she covered him up, he talked so much and put on such an act that Mrs Rudd's nerves got the better of her, she couldn't stand it, and then he grabbed Dad's fingernail and tore it right out so she had to send him to the Zoo. Mrs Rudd went to the Zoo and stood by the cockies' cage and one came up to her and said, 'What's cooking, good looking?' and she knew it was Old Bill straight away.

Mrs Tidy lived next door on the other side, and if I went to the shop for her, she'd give me a penny. I worried about losing my money so I carried it in my shoe. There were a lot of shops round the corner in Hindley Street, a whole row of them.

The pig's head in the butcher's window had a lemon stuck in its mouth; Mr Crist, the chemist, sold the Zac cough-medicine we took for colds; Mr Pianto, the grocer, was Italian – but white Italian, he had blue eyes. There was a fireworks shop where you bought all kinds of crackers and wheels and bombs for Fire Day; a photographer's, where I posed with my hand on a fancy carved chair and my brother was taken holding a whip; a tailor's, where men sat sewing, cross-legged, on a table and I was given enough samples of suit materials to make a patchwork rug for my brother's bed because he was a beggar for dirtying his white quilt. A lady, a real old-fashioned type, sold tobacco and cigarettes and lollies and cotton – anything that anybody might want in a hurry. Another lady, called Frenchy, wore a tomato-coloured wig with curls and a bow at the back; she smelt of Dew of Violets scent but she wasn't pretty. Frenchy's shop window always had its curtains drawn, because only her boyfriends entered the shop at night. Mrs Tidy said to Mum that men didn't care what she looked like, as long as they got what they wanted. There was a Chinaman whose shop was a workroom; he was a carpenter and he gave me wood shavings. I tied the long curls round my head with string, then put on a hat, and they were like sausage curls down my back. Other kids sang out 'Ching Chong Chinaman' and all that sort of thing. I never cheeked anybody, I just liked people.

[5]

At the Observation and Practising School in Currie Street the boys were fenced off, they couldn't come into the girls' part; there was a gate but it had to be kept shut and they had men teachers, we had lady teachers.

My first teacher in the kindergarten was Little Miss Watson, who was short, and when I went into the next class we had another Miss Watson, who was nothing to do with the first one. She was tall, so we called her Big Miss Watson, and she made us sing in the morning 'Good morning, dear teacher'. All round the wall were blackboards, and each girl had one to herself where she had to draw or write or do whatever was supposed to be done. I didn't have to learn very much because Dad had already taught me the alphabet and my numbers, and he made a piece of cardboard into a clock and turned the hands and asked me what time it was.

Miss Vaux had black hair and rather a yellowish skin; when we went into her class, work really began. But I talked a terrible lot, Miss Vaux said she'd never heard anyone talk as much as I did, so she stood me behind the door and once she even sent me into the boys' class to see if Mr Saunders could do anything with me; but I was only there half an hour because I disrupted the boys. We had *The Adelaide Copy Book* and *McDougall's Sensible Speller* and we drew the passion-flower leaf in lead pencil and bisected an arc; there was a poem called 'The Orphan's Recollections of a Mother' and we learnt about St George, King Alfred, Dr Livingstone and Handy Weights and Measures. Miss Vaux took her holidays in foreign places and brought back costumes for the girls to wear in her concerts – only the girls in the front row of the concert, because she couldn't supply clothes for them all. They wore the proper clogs with the Dutch costumes, and then she'd have a Japanese concert with fans and kimonos and everything. I was never dressed up, I don't know why.

Miss Holman was a dear, you could just about twist her round your finger. But sometimes we played up a bit and she'd blush to the back teeth and have to leave the room and come back when she was composed.

Mum boiled meat and saved me the knucklebones to play with at recess. I played marbles and could skip with two ropes going – bob down and skip at the same time, then stand up again and keep skipping and never stop the ropes. We did the maypole dance, not in the dead of winter or the heat of summer, but in the maypole season. The tuck shop across the road made beautiful pies – you could get other pies, but they weren't in the same show; and I bought Kali suckers, liquorice straps, milk chocolate stars. Sometimes there

17

were special events when we marched through the gate into the boys' yard and I saw my brother playing the kettledrum in the school band. The Governors' ladies came to see us and Lady Galway held her hands up to her chest to clap and just tapped on her fingers, it was a ladylike way of clapping but it looked silly. And there was one called Lady Weigall, who wasn't very popular; she thought the working class should wear only navy and red, so people would know who they were.

[6]

Sunday was bath day and after I had my dinner I put on my best dress and went to Holy Trinity Sunday School. My teacher was the minister's daughter and she admired Mum's crochetwork, so Mum gave her two doilies in case she got married.

We sang:

> *Dropping, dropping, dropping,*
> *Hear the pennies fall,*
> *Every one for Jesus,*
> *He shall have them all*

as we put our pennies in the box for collection. They liked having my brother at Sunday School because he sang out above the other voices. He had a very strong voice and was quite a good singer, but I hated him singing with me because I couldn't hear myself.

Esther Weinig used to wait outside Holy Trinity till

Sunday School was over and then we'd walk down to the river past the river-policeman's house. He had a walnut tree in his garden that hung over the footpath. When the walnuts were green we'd knock some off with a stick and fill our pockets; Mum preferred them green, when their insides were like jelly. Once we saw men dragging the river both sides of the bridge and then they pulled a boy who'd been drowned out of the reeds. He was all swollen from being in the water.

Weinigs said they were Scots Jews. Mrs Weinig was born in Scotland, certainly, and they ate bread like thin cake on Jewish occasions, but Mr Weinig was born in Russia. He went out to Scotland to get away from the Russians, and she picked him up. She'd been married before and got all her money from the husband that died. Old Weinig never had anything; she had the money, and when they came to Australia she filled her children's pockets and clothes with gold sovereigns and draped bags of sovereigns round them on account of the Customs. Weinigs had a nice house in Hindley Street and a wash woman to come in and do the washing and a summer house at Mount Lofty with the bedrooms upstairs, but she was a real little Scots woman who ruled the roost.

Samuel, Abraham, Nathan and Jacob were the four sons; Celia, Cis, Esther and Ruth were the four daughters. Celia and Cis, Mrs Weinig's children by her first husband, had ginger hair but all the others had black and looked alike. Celia took after her mother and bossed the kids. Cis went to work as a maid for a high toff in North Adelaide and one of the sons got her into trouble. The baby was the dead spit of her with ginger hair, and he had manners just like a gentleman. Samuel and Abraham worked in Mr Weinig's hardware shop, Nathan was called Nacky. He was a devil, never home; he just took off, went over to Melbourne and lived on money he'd pinched from his mother until it was all gone and his clothes were worn out – then he'd write and tell her that he was stranded.

Esther was in my class at school; she was a very talkative girl, worse than me, and if I wanted to say something I had to break into her conversation. Sometimes we went into the brewery in Hindley Street to see what was going on and talk to the men – we knew them all and called them by their Christian names. The brewery horses were given beer to drink; their coats shone like anything, they had brass medallions and usually four white feet. If we had a penny to spend, we'd go to Pianto's and choose from halfpenny ice-creams and glasses of lemonade; milk poles that you could chew on for ages, liquorice straps and curls.

On Saturday afternoons Esther and I went to the pictures to see Mary Pickford, and once Mrs Weinig said we had to take Ruth but we didn't want her – she was too young, she was a darned nuisance as far as we were concerned. Mrs Weinig wrapped up Ruth's admission money separately and gave it to me because I was the tallest, but going along Hindley Street I lost it down a grating. When we got to the theatre I bought

Esther's ticket and mine, and then took off my coat and wrapped Ruth up and tried to carry her in. While I was struggling with her, the chap on the door asked where her ticket was and I said, 'She's a child in arms.' He laughed and said he'd never seen anything so well got up and let us in.

Jacob was the nicest looking Weinig and he asked Mum if she'd allow me to go with him to watch a procession in town for the War. There were decorated lorries and people in costumes collecting and Jacob brought me home safe and sound, but an hour afterwards he was killed at the Mile End crossing. He was smashed to pieces by a train and they had to shovel him up. Esther came and told us and Mum went straight round to console Mrs Weinig.

Mrs Weinig was so upset she couldn't go to the funeral, but she had special cards made with a verse and Jacob's photo on them. There were lots of flowers and the hearse was glassed-in so you could see the coffin. Esther often put flowers on Jacob's grave on her way to church – she went to church on a Saturday because they were Jewish.

[7]

South Australia's soldiers marched away with bunches of wattle pinned to their tunics. Kangaroos were regimental pets in some of the transport waggons; one soldier nursed a great bulldog framed in Union Jacks.

Because of the War, there was always something going on in the city. A man sat in a glass cabinet outside Catt's drapery store in Rundle Street and people gave a coin for the Patriotic Fund and guessed how long he could stay there without eating and drinking (but it was a bit of a fake because his buttons were covered in chocolate and when no one was looking he'd suck them for nourishment). Another time, Catt's had a big candle in the cabinet and people guessed how long it would burn. There were button days, concerts, cat and dog shows; garden fêtes with decorated umbrella competitions and the Tramways Band played a Hungarian waltz to aid the Belgian Relief Fund. When there was a procession I'd hop on to one of the lorries and try to collect some money for the soldiers. A popular patriotic worker called Sammy Lunn dressed up in evening clothes and swang his walking-stick as he sang and danced on the steps of the Grand picture theatre. One day I got talking to him and the next thing he had me singing and dancing, too, while people clapped and threw coins.

I saw lantern slides illustrating the War in France, Egypt, Palestine and Gallipoli; an Englishman called George Olds stayed in my brother's room for a few weeks before he went overseas with his regiment; I knitted socks for the soldiers but I couldn't turn the heels, so Dorrie did them for me.

Men were going off to be heroes with fixed bayonets as enthusiastic ladies showered them with flowers, and other men stood like chimney-pots on the tops of buildings and cheered. When George Olds went he left his Bible and civilian clothes with us and said he'd send for them when the War was over. Mrs Fry's son went, and her two daughters' husbands.

Mum's friend, Mrs Fry, lived on the corner of our street in a big house with a broad staircase and a small garden out the front and a fig tree at the back. Once Mrs Fry stood on a box to pick some figs and fell off and broke her arm; she must have had brittle bones.

I'd go into the big house and set the table and put the kettle on and Mrs Fry would be so pleased to think she didn't have to rush about to get things ready for tea. When they came in to have their meal, I'd play waitress and carry the plates round and Mrs Fry would dish up a plateful for me. On Saturday nights they had fancy cream cakes and I thought it was lovely.

Mrs Fry's daughter, Lottie, was a dressmaker with a sewing-room off the kitchen. She made me a stiff white organdie dress for summer and a black velvet one for winter. I just about lived in her workroom. I tidied things away and picked up pins with a horseshoe magnet, but I never touched her sewing-machine. Lottie gave me scraps of material and any ends of lace she didn't want.

The other daughter, Nell, kept her hair in curls by bathing it with the yolk of a new laid egg beaten up in a pint of warm rainwater before going to bed.

Every Saturday morning I pushed Mrs Fry's cart to the market for her. On the way, we often saw the man with the performing dogs that walked on their front paws with their back legs up in the air and did all sorts of other tricks. A blindman sat by the bank and played the concertina, and knew which people passed him by their footsteps. Mrs Fry gave me a penny for the chocolate machine where you got a dog's head printed on a card with the chocolate, and if you got No. 1 dog's head it was very lucky; I got all the others of the set, but I never got No. 1 dog's head. Sometimes we saw the old woman who wore a lot of veils down over her face, and always carried a billy-can and an umbrella; she wouldn't pay when she rode on the trams – she'd hit the conductor on the head if he tried to make her.

When we reached the market Mrs Fry went off with the cart to choose what she wanted. I watched the man called Johnny Allsorts at the secondhand stall, and there was a cheapjack that was only threepence a go – you pulled a ticket out and whatever was on it you won; Mrs Fry won a goose once, and I had to carry it home. Sometimes I went to help a man serve on one of the fruit stalls and when it was time for me to go, he'd give me a big paper bag and tell me to fill it with whatever fruit I fancied.

Mrs Fry took Esther Weinig and me to the beach. We went down in a horse and cart with the tent and the lunch baskets while Lottie and Nell went in the train. Men swam to one side of the jetty and ladies to the other. The men's bathers had short sleeves and long pants, they were cotton and clung. Some of the ladies had skirts on their bathers, for modesty's sake.

People rode horses on the damp sand at the edge of

the sea. There were sideshows on the esplanade and you paid sixpence to see the sword swallower and the man who wore a suit of writhing snakes and the man prepared to tie his body in a knot for a silver coin. A performing monkey was dressed up like a bell-boy in a scarlet coat and pants and a little round hat; you could tumble two men into a tub of water if you hit the bull's-eye. The American chair-balancer risked death by performing on the roof garden of the Pier Hotel.

[8]

Every Monday evening when Dad worked late, Mum and I went to the pictures at the Grand. When we were watching *Madonna of the Night*, the manager appeared on the stage to announce that the Armistice had been signed and the audience went wild with joy. Women wept, became hysterical, and a few even fainted.

Bells rang, whistles blew, the streets were packed with people; there were tin-can bands, brass bands, and thousands of voices sang patriotic songs. Newsboys selling special editions yelled, 'Peace declared!' Sailors and soldiers were hoisted shoulder-high; daring spirits scrambled on the roofs of trams and performed sand dances. Sammy Lunn led a contingent of merrymakers, all cheering, singing and shouting to the Town Hall.

People stuffed old suits with straw to make effigies of the Kaiser and the Crown Prince to burn during the Peace Celebrations, while the British Jack flew from the flagpole at Government House. There was a great demonstration on the Adelaide Oval by twelve thousand school-children (omitting those of tender years), and we were given a holiday from school and a Peace medal.

George Olds had been killed in France and his clothes were getting moth-eaten so Mum burnt them, but I kept his Bible. Because Mrs Fry's son came back from the War with a sex disease, his wife tried to get rid of the baby when she became pregnant, but couldn't, so she jumped off a wall and died soon after. Lottie's husband came back with a leg off and a stump in its place; he wore an artificial leg, but it was awkward as the stump was so short. Nell's husband came back stone-deaf because he'd worked on the cannons and a German shell blew his cannon to pieces; he was thrown to the ground while all the other men were killed and he never got his hearing back. He was always down in Mrs Fry's cellar making pedestals and little tables with curved legs. He taught me to punch a medicine ball shaped like a pear and we played dominoes because he couldn't hear the calls to play cards.

[9]

Granma McGregor lived in Scotland with Aunt Maggie and Uncle Jock. When Mum and Dad were first married she came out to South Africa to visit them but she found fault with everything Mum did, even the way she wound her balls of knitting wool. Dad had a photo of Granma McGregor with her hair done like Queen Mary's, all little curls piled up, and she had bones in her high collars and sat with a fur rug over her legs. She got on Mum's nerves. Dad kept the photo in their bedroom but Mum was always hiding it away.

Dad steamed off the stamps from Granma's letters and stuck them in his album. One day Aunt Maggie wrote and told him of Granma's death. She left some money to Dad and he put it towards buying a house in Rose Street, Thebarton, an old suburb close to the city.

But we couldn't shift because I was sick. I'd caught flu in the epidemic of 1919, when thousands died overseas and people in Adelaide wore masks in the street and camphor bags round their necks and the tram windows were kept open to circulate air so travellers wouldn't become infected.

When I got up from bed I was so weak that I couldn't even turn the knob of the door to let myself out, but I'd started getting better so we shifted. Every house that had a severe case of flu had to have a yellow flag on a stick in the front garden. We'd only been in the new house a couple of days when a flag went up next door, and Mum worried that I might catch the flu again.

They put my bed in the dining-room and lit the fire and I took things easy. The balloon-legged table from the old house was there, and the chairs with curly-bearded faces that pressed against you when you leant back. On the sideboard was a model of a boiler that Dad had made out of copper. When he heated it up on the gas stove in the kitchen, steam whistled from its chimney as a tiny pressure-gauge went round.

I looked at the picture of a country scene on the wall and pretended it was where Mum had lived in South Africa . . . and the English soldiers aimed their rifles and the Boer women were shot tied to chairs, the lions in the hills roared, Granpa walked ten paces behind his daughters when they went to dances, Dorrie was given away to a black woman, Aunt Lily was artistic and painted a flower garden round the hem of Mum's dance dress but she died of diphtheria the same day as her girlfriend so they had a double funeral, Mum's pet monkey sat on a cocky-stand with a chain round his leg and his cheeks puffed out as he stuffed them with grapes, the black men put diamonds up their back passages, Uncle John was a devil, Mum saw zebras and elephants, she had a silver leaf from Table Mountain.

They gave me the box of photos from South Africa . . . a tame bear, his own great big brown bear, it was taller than him and in the photo he was a smart young man with a moustache and a riding crop; it was a performing bear with a chain round its neck and the young man wore high boots and a jumper (they didn't dress up in collar and tie to train their animals); *To Anna from William* was written in best copperplate on the back of the photo, Mum was engaged to him but changed her mind. And Granpa Duret sat in his chair in the garden under the creeper with leaves like flags; bearded, looking fierce, as if he never laughed, the big house behind him with six front windows. And in

28

another photo he sat stiffly on the front verandah with his friend – both in top-hats, a round table with a teapot between them; and at the edge of the photo, facing the camera, stood a little black boy, neatly dressed (he had to keep his back to the gentlemen until they called for more tea). And Mum wore a grey dress and an ostrich feather cape when she married Dad in a Dutch Reformed church – it was her wedding photo (but she gave the cape to a lady on the steamer to Australia and sold the knives, forks and spoons with grapevines on their handles she got as a wedding present). At the bottom of the box was Granma Duret's purple silk Bible marker and her satin and ivory folding fan, hand-painted with sprays of flowers.

[10]

The new house had electric light and a pantry that was cool enough for the jellies to set. Mum didn't like the wallpaper in her bedroom, even though it had pink flowers and silver dots that stood out; she got Dorrie and Tom to take all the paper off and kalsomine the walls white. She had the kitchen painted blue and there was a red cloth with a fringe on the table. When Dad wanted to read his books and there was too much gossip in the kitchen, he'd go to the bedroom and shut the door and lie on the bed.

Down the centre of the back yard, by the path to the tap, was a grape trellis with black and white muscatels and lady's-fingers. On one side was a great big apricot tree and sometimes when I climbed it, the girl next door would climb her fig tree and we'd step over the fence into each other's tree, because she wanted to eat apricots and I wanted to eat figs. On the other side of the trellis, shaded by a nectarine tree from the afternoon sun, was a strawberry patch and we made a little gutter and left the tap dripping, so the water would run to the strawberries. Beyond that, by the fowl house, Mum grew broad beans and then a fence of wire-netting covered in lavatory creeper divided the top part of the yard from the bottom, that was just tall green grass.

One day I saw a swarm of bees settling on the creeper, so I fixed up a box on the netting with a dish of water inside; when the queen flew in all the others followed. I gave them fresh water every day and they started to build three cones of wax filled with honey. I'd put my hand in, but I never got stung, and if any bees had died I'd pick them out and bury them and hang a wreath of creeper over the cross on their grave. Once Mum looked in the box and was stung on the eyelid, but I could see the stinger and hooked it out with my fingers. In the end, we took the cones from the box and broke the wax seal, drained the honey into a basin and put it in the pantry.

Our fowls were black Orpingtons, white Leghorns and Highland reds. Dad built an incubator and when it was in use it was kept in my brother's bedroom and Tom wasn't allowed to walk heavily, because it would disturb the eggs. They were turned every day and I'd often tiptoe in to look through the glass to see if the chickens were coming out. When they did, they were all wet, in a bunch; Dad put them in the top compartment and then, as they grew stronger, they went into the brooder on the back verandah. They ran round in one part and slept in the other, under strips of flannel that hung from the lid in rows to make a false mother.

We had a snow-white cat, a little Persian, but it died in the bath – it picked up a bait and went into the bathroom and lay under the dripping tap; I supposed its stomach was hot through whatever poison it had eaten. I bought some pigeons at the market and brought them home in a box on the tram, though you weren't meant to carry birds on board; my brother made a cage to keep them in, but I got tired of pigeons and let them go. I kept silkworms in a shoe box with holes punched in the lid and fed them on mulberry leaves and wound up the yellow silk.

The leaves came from an old man who lived down the street, across from the Thebarton School. When he knew school was coming out, he'd pick them and be waiting with them at his gate. I'd stop and have a talk and tell him all the things that had happened to me and then he'd tell me about old times. He'd been born on one of the pioneer ships and carried ashore by the bosun; he remembered Thebarton when it was just a wheat paddock.

I started to learn the piano from Miss Phelps, who lived in Kintore Street. She kept house for her sister and did piano teaching after school and on Saturdays. Once when I went for my lesson, a boy was there doing his theory; he hated theory and I hated playing scales, so when Miss Phelps went out of the room we changed places. I got halfway through his theory and he was playing away, but his touch was heavier than mine and Miss Phelps came back and caught us.

We didn't have a piano, so I practised next door in Pobjoys'. Mr Pobjoy shifted scenes for the plays at the Theatre Royal. Pobjoys' girl who climbed the fig tree was older than me and ran after boyfriends. The electricity had been disconnected because the bills hadn't been paid, but Mr Pobjoy started using it again with wires hooked up in all the rooms, looped down the passage and everywhere. The Electric Light Company found out and a man came to our house asking questions; I didn't know I was supposed to keep my mouth shut and told him Pobjoys had the light on when I practised. I had to stand up in the witness box at Court and swear on the Bible, so Pobjoys didn't speak to us and I stopped learning the piano.

Our neighbours on the other side were the Mackies; she was a Catholic, but he wasn't and was always running them down. They had itchy-pod trees, bamboos and a fishpond in their front garden. Mum gave me her old lace curtains and I sewed a bridesmaid's dress for little Mary Mackie out of one, and a wedding dress for me out of the other, but I never bothered with a veil. I curled up Mary's hair in rags, we both had bunches of flowers, and Mrs Mackie said we were as pure as the angels in heaven. Then the Mackies went off to Western Australia and the Borchers came to live there. Mrs Borchers showed us photos of her old home in Germany, where she'd been somebody because Mr Borchers had been so high up in the military. Their house wasn't much, now, just a brick box with a latticed porch, but he wanted to start a cooperage in the big back yard. Mrs Borchers had a folding screen patterned with mother-of-pearl peacocks; she was artistic and scrubbed her sitting-room floor spotless, then painted it with bunches of flowers, just like lino, and you were frightened to walk on it.

Mr Willoughby, who lived further up the street, was lame and had a wood yard; he organized the bonfire in the paddock across the road when it was Guy Fawkes' Night. Boys fought in Willoughby's paddock after school, the milkman kept his cows there, and I'd cut across it every week to get to the Beach Road to buy my comic paper. *Bubbles* was running a serial about a boy and girl who lived in a windmill and Flahertys' girl, who went to the convent, bought *Puck*, that had a serial, too. We'd each read our episode as fast as we could, then change over, so she could read the *Bubbles* serial and I could read the *Puck*. One day, coming back through the paddock, reading *Bubbles*, I fell over one of the cows.

[11]

For a while after I recovered from the flu, I went back to the Observation School. I was supposed to catch the tram into the city each day but, instead, I walked all the way and spent my tram-fare money on lollies. Mum got wind of it and bought me a tram pass, then decided to send me to the Thebarton School.

Miss O'Hara, my teacher, was a Catholic who decorated her table with green ribbons on St Patrick's Day. She was an old thing who always had a cane, she should have been pensioned off. When my needle disappeared in sewing lesson, she put on such an act that it might have been a sovereign I'd lost. I thought if I could sweeten her up she'd like me better, so I lined a box with vine leaves, then picked the nicest strawberries I could find in the garden, packed them in and put more vine leaves over the top. I gave them to her at school and she told me next day she'd made a strawberry tart and had it with cream. After the strawberries I was *it*, and even sat at her table and took over when she had to leave the classroom.

My next teacher was Miss Jarvis, who was sarcastic. She was always whirling the globe of the world round, asking questions, but whenever I put my hand up to answer one she just looked at me, then picked someone else; if she said anything to me, she had a sarcastic way of saying it. Miss Jarvis taught us flower painting and I didn't like daisies but made a good job of fuchsia sprays

34

and I'd pick up a few violets, just drop them on the desk, then freehand draw them very fine. But Miss Jarvis took my flower paintings and wouldn't give them back.

Once I wore my best madapollam petticoat hemmed with crochetwork in diamond pattern to school, instead of my usual calico one. I lifted my skirt up when I sat down at my desk, so the other girls could see it; I got a shock when I took it off at home that night, because the girl who sat behind me in sewing had snipped off all the crocheted diamonds at the back with her scissors.

I sat next to Audrey at school. Her father owned a rope-works and always gave her the Pope's nose when it was roast chicken for Sunday dinner. Audrey wore silk stockings over her cashmere ones, because she liked the silky look, and next year she was going to the Methodist Ladies' College. She could sing a Scots song with very high notes; she had a little pug nose and fair curly hair but she didn't want long hair because everybody was wearing it short, so one night she got up and cut it all off, left it on the floor with the scissors, and went back to bed. In the morning, her mother thought she must have done it in her sleep; Audrey didn't tell her any different and her mother took her to a doctor.

Audrey came over to my place after school and we used to lie in the grass at the bottom of the yard and tell secrets; once Mr Willoughby stuck his head over the fence and asked if we'd seen the snake he'd been chasing.

I was playing cricket in the yard and suddenly felt

sticky; I kept going inside to wash myself, but the next minute I'd feel sticky again. Mum had never told me anything and when I saw the blood I told Dorrie, who gave me a piece of old sheet to wear. I hated wearing it to school, you sat so long it felt dry and horrible.

When I fainted at school, Elsie Abbott, whose father had the barber's on the Beach Road, caught me as I fell. Miss Jarvis asked me if I had my pain and said whenever it came not to join in marching or drilling. I hated marching and drilling, so when we had to do them, whether I had it or not, I'd go and sit under the pepper tree in the school-yard.

[12]

The house in Rose Street was sold to a policeman and we shifted round the corner to Pearl Street, one of the oldest streets in Thebarton. It was narrow, with a gasometer up one end and some of the pioneers' little low cottages were still there. I went in the cart with the furniture; I sat up in front beside the driver and took over the reins while he had a smoke.

Our new house was the nicest we'd had, with roses, a rockery, a fern house and a coprosma hedge with shiny leaves that Dad paid me conscience money to keep trimmed. There was a trellis of grapevines from the back fence to the verandah – muscatels, sweet-waters, lady's-fingers. There was a tree that didn't have fruit; Mum thought it was an apple tree, but Dad said pear; it came out in blossom after I climbed up on the fowl house and pruned it, and then we had so many big rosy Statesman apples that we didn't know what to do with them. There was a lemon tree that my brother used to sit under and nurse the hens and one laid an egg in his lap.

Mum had her photo taken in a dark blue suit, a long string of pearls and a blouse that had rows and rows of lace. She hung it in an oval frame on the sitting-room wall over the fireplace, between two paintings of a pair of swans, each swimming towards her. On the mantelpiece was a brass jardinière embossed with grapes and usually filled with flowers. Mum didn't like white flowers, so when white lilies were all she had, she painted pink stripes on them with lipstick.

Dad bought a phonograph in a walnut cabinet and some records. We had Harry Lauder, and Caruso singing 'Beneath Thy Window'. Dad played his piano-accordion and we'd dance in the dining-room where there was lino and not a lot of mats. We'd do the Alberts, the Lancers, 'The Bonnie Scotland Waltz', but Mum wouldn't dance because Granma Duret, on her death-bed, made her promise not to. My brother wasn't a bad dancer but he didn't like slow waltzes, only quick steps, and was always in a hurry.

The Salvation Army band played out the front by the electric-light post on Sunday evenings; Waltons, who lived at the back, had a loquat tree; Mr Walton was a dentist's mechanic, Mrs Walton had a pet magpie that once pecked her in the eye. The man across the road's eyes had been blown out in the mines at Broken Hill and his wife was colour-blind. Next to the blind people was Mrs Sullivan, a queer old tart who was always coming back from the Wheatsheaf Hotel with flaggons of wine; Mrs Sullivan's son murdered her one night and people thought she was a bundle of clothes lying in the gutter. Mr Prisk, the cabinetmaker, who lived on the corner, was the first man in the street to have a car; his yard was full of fruit trees and vines but he'd rather see the fruit rot than give it away. All the Daleys had ginger hair and lived in the row of attached cottages. Old Mr Daley was ninety-four, with a few ginger strands in his white beard and a holly tree in his garden; he sat out on the footpath in his chair because he was fond of the children and liked them to run round him.

Mrs Lemon, next door, was a little woman, a happy type; she was practically stone-deaf and didn't know what was going on. Mr Lemon, who worked for the Council as a dustman, was always rousing and beat his grown-up children with his felt hat, girls and all. When the eldest Lemon boy had gone off to the War he'd given his father permission to put his army pay in the bank for him, so he'd have a few hundred saved up for when he came home to marry his girlfriend. But Mr Lemon was so mean he cheated his son and used the money to build a new brick house in front of the tumble-down cottage the family had been living in. Lemons had a prickly cactus in their garden that hung over our fence; Mum didn't like it, so she crept out one night and poured kerosene round its roots and it died.

Next door to us on the other side was a paddock where the bottleoh kept his draught horses. They'd come to the fence and I'd talk to them as I scratched their noses, and fed them sugar cubes and apples cut into quarters. I loved to feel the horses' lips on my hand – just like velvet, soft as soft.

The baker called each day with his loaves in a wicker basket lined with white tea-towels and the bread smelt beautiful, you felt you had to eat it straight away. There was the greengrocer, the rabbit-man, the Terai-tea man, the Chinese pedlar with his little boxes hanging from a pole across his shoulders. In summer the ice-man came with a block of ice in his grips and Mr Twist rang his bell and drove about the streets in his cart, selling the nicest ice-cream you ever tasted. In winter the river often flooded and water ran through the front doors of houses. People lined the Port Road bridge to watch trees and dead animals float past, and fished for fruit and vegetables that had been swept away from gardens in the Hills.

[13]

Dorrie's first steady boyfriend was Arthur, a French-polisher, who lived on the Bay line and belonged to the walkers. He showed me how to walk on the balls of my feet and I won the walking race at the Sunday School picnic – the prize was a jar of Alpine Snow face cream.

Arthur made Dorrie a highly-polished jewel box,

39

padded inside with pink silk. It had a proper lock and key and Dorrie kept her watch, bangles and brooches in it.

Dorrie had two Bills. She was walking along the street with the first one who was a Catholic, when he suddenly knelt down in front of a church and started crossing himself, so she walked off and caught the tram home. Then there was Bill Charlick; Dorrie hated his straight hair, so I gave him a kiss-curl in front with my curling-tongs. But Bill lost his father and had to support his mother and brothers and sisters; it didn't seem there'd be any prospects, so Dorrie broke it off.

I had no intention of interfering with Dorrie's love life, but I was very pally with Claude, the next one. I showed him what I wrote in bed when I woke up early. I was always reading the Bible and I'd started writing about Bible-times – not so much about Bible knowledge, as far as God was concerned, but about the people who were living then. I wrote pages and pages on all the leading ones, I tried to make a story round it; Claude was the only person I ever showed it to.

Dorrie left Bottomley's to work at the Perfection Shirt Factory in Hindmarsh Square; when I was fourteen she got me a job there, too. Mum bought me a pair of stays and I wore them the first morning, but they were so uncomfortable I couldn't breathe. I took them off in the lavatory and sold them to Dorrie for a pound.

The Perfection made pyjamas as well as shirts, and was owned by Mr Laverti, an Englishman with a smooth complexion and a stiff collar and tie, though he took his coat off when he was cutting out. He tried to make me feel at home, but I was afraid of him; when he spoke I thought he was going to eat me.

There were thirty girls working in a big room filled with the sound of electric machines. I started on the finishing table, where the girls cut off the ends of threads, and we'd talk and carry on. I was the youngest, so I had to get the lunches and Mr Laverti had a ham sandwich every day. It was quite a walk with my basket to the shop in Grenfell Street, but I didn't mind because I was outside, walking round the city. I brought such a big order that I could have the pick of the shop without paying; one day I'd choose a chicken sandwich, the next ham, and I always had a little sponge cake with a dob of raspberry jam and a whole heap of cream.

After a while I went on the button machine to sew buttons on the shirts and pyjamas. It had a foot with a slit in it that held the button firm, and when you pressed the treadle the needle came down to sew it on. The buttons were in boxes – good pearl buttons for the fashion shirts, common ones for working shirts, bigger ones for the pyjamas.

Valerie, who worked the buttonhole machine, couldn't keep away from boys; she was a devil, though she came from a good home. She wore lipstick and plucked her eyebrows and came in every morning with a yarn about going down the park or round the gardens with boys and having it. She dressed well and the girls said that probably the boys paid her – she wouldn't have got that much money on the buttonhole machine.

When Valerie finished putting the buttonholes in, she hung the shirt over a clothes-horse and then the forelady stuck her pencil through the holes and marked where the buttons went. She called Valerie and me Stiffy and Mo (she never said it in a nasty way, it was just her way of speaking), after the famous comics who acted at the Majestic. Mo was short and did his face up to look silly; Stiffy was tall. The forelady was always trying to straighten Valerie out – she even took her to the pictures to keep her away from the boys. But Valerie was a good worker. She worked like mad, till she'd cleared everything off, and then she'd want to talk.

Mr Laverti cut out the pyjamas and dress shirts and specials; Arnold, a nice clean fresh boy the girls whispered about, cut out the working shirts and the button-down ones. The pieces of material were piled high, the pattern laid down and drawn round, then the big cutting machine cut in and out. Then Arnold counted the pieces into bundles, tied them up, and the forelady gave them to the girls.

All the girls had their different jobs. Each machinist sat on a chair with a cushion, a clothes-horse beside her. The machines went down the middle of the room – flat machines, two-needle machines that sewed the seams neatly, the buttonhole and button machines. To one side were the cutting tables; to the other, the finishing table. The three collar-hands – Flo, Kath, Miss Stanley – were Dorrie's friends. Four girls pressed the shirts and pyjamas, then pinned them up; they were packed into boxes and the shops came to collect them in their vans.

There were fashion shirts with tailored sleeves and gauntlet cuffs in neat silk pencil-stripes; strong-wearing black Italian-cloth working shirts; Oxford twill cricketing and tennis shirts. The pyjamas were winter-weight winceyette or striped cotton or Fuji silk: splendid wearing, cool and comfortable, best make and finish, double-sewn throughout, nice and roomy. If a man wanted a special shirt made, he brought his own material and was measured by Mr Laverti in his office. Dorrie did all the specials, even the dress shirts with little pleats, and sometimes pin-tucks, down the front. She was a fast worker and Mr Laverti had wanted her to be the forelady, but she wouldn't take it on. She said she was too friendly with the girls.

[14]

Everybody called my brother Mac, though his name was Tom. He asked me why I didn't call him Mac, too, and I said, 'You're Tom to me and you'll stay Tom.' He was six feet tall and well built, with a dimple in his chin and Mum's dark brown eyes. He was the quickest eater you ever came across, no matter how much you put on his plate he always finished first – but he never ate meat, only vegetables. When he was dressed up in his best suit and silk shirt, a velour hat and patent leather shoes, you would have thought him a real man about town. He had a cut-throat razor that he kept in his cedar chest of drawers; he only had to shave on his chin and I said he should grow a goatee beard like a Frenchman.

Once Tom worked at a motorbike shop on the Beach Road and took the brand new bike out of the window when the boss was on holiday; he rode it round the Hills all day, then cleaned it up and put it back again. After Tom learnt engineering at the School of Mines, he went to big stores and factories installing systems that would sprinkle water if there was a fire. When he slipped off a roof at Holdens, he landed on his feet but his right eye was never the same.

Someone put a cocky in a cage over our fence and when Dorrie and I came home from the Perfection, everyone was in the back yard trying to entice him out. Mum tried, Dad tried, Tom tried with a rag round his hand because he was frightened it would bite him and still the cocky wouldn't leave the cage. I said Tom would never do it like that, because birds could feel fear. I put my hand in the cage and said, 'Come on, cocky,' and he perched on my finger and I brought him out. I'd talk to him and he liked a little shower, so I'd gently spray him with the hose.

I introduced Tom to Molly Dick, who'd been in my class at school, and he started going out with her. The Dicks were quite a family – there were six daughters and one son called Dick Dick. I was a great one for introducing people and after I introduced Mrs Dick to Mum, every other week there was a ladies' evening at our place or Dicks'.

Dick Dick's wife used to get Mum to mind the baby while she carried on with a barman at the Land of Promise Hotel; Dick Dick found out and gave her a hiding.

Sometimes when Dad was reading in bed and Dorrie and Tom were out, Mum and I had supper. Dad said, 'You'll dream of the devil,' when I made scones or stickjaw toffee that you could pull a mile long; or I'd mix up a fairly firm batter, drop spoonfuls in hot fat, and they'd come out puffed up like balls. We'd split them open and put anything we liked in them – butter, honey, golden syrup.

Tom stopped going out with Molly Dick because she turned out to be a bit sexy. He told Mum he got an awful shock – Molly took his hand and put it between her legs. Mum was disgusted.

[15]

After the button machine tried to stitch a button on to my finger, and the forelady had to pull the needle out with her teeth, I left the Perfection for one of the sewing rooms at Moore's, the big department store in Victoria Square. I went to work on a cup of tea, I didn't need breakfast because I had a cream cake at ten o'clock. I worked from eight o'clock to a quarter to six, for the shop opened for customers, so we had to come in the side door by the arcade.

They made dresses in the sewing room upstairs, but I was in the basement where we made bloomers and blouses and overalls and once we even made shrouds for the nuns in the convent to be buried in. They had hoods and a blue cross of ribbon down the front; I dressed up in one and pretended to be dead, but Miss Gibson, the forelady, caught me.

Miss Gibson was a big woman who kept herself smart and well-dressed and supplied us with needles, pins and cotton. We had to bring our own scissors and tape-measures and it was hard sitting on a wooden chair all day, so we brought our own cushions, too. We wore aprons, but took them off when we went to the lavatory, because there were always men from the Dispatch Department in the passage – you never knew who you might meet.

At first Miss Gibson put me on the finishing table, where I cut off threads and did hand-sewing and beading. There were boxes of beads and you tacked a transfer to a blouse and where there was a dash you sewed a bugle bead and where there wasn't, a seed bead. Or you sewed bunches of seed beads for the centres of flowers, bugle beads for their petals, and if it was a blouse for an older person it was all done in black. Then Miss Gibson put me at the ironing table but I wasn't used to standing on my legs, pressing for hours. I got so tired she asked me to make a buttonhole and I did it better than anyone else, so then I made button-holes all day.

We were allowed ten minutes every day to go shopping in the store – but only two girls at a time. I went round the departments, I made friends with most of the assistants. Tom was always looking for tall girls and when he came to Moore's to install the sprinkler system, I introduced him to Myra who worked in the Underwear and won the competition for the best legs at the Waterworks picnic.

Hazel worked on the button counter, and I'd get up early to meet her in the morning on the Beach Road and we'd cross the railway line and walk through the parklands to work. One morning at the Mile End crossing, where Jacob Weinig had been killed, a man was smashed to pieces. There were blood spots everywhere and we saw men picking up bits of his body and putting them in a sugar bag. But they forgot an arm – it wasn't a very big arm, it wouldn't have been any bigger than my own.

When I was sixteen, I pierced my ears. I did it in my brother's bedroom, because his cedar chest of drawers had a mirror on top and there was a light over it so I could see what I was doing. It didn't hurt much. My right ear was the worst, because I had to do it left-handed; I made the hole in the wrong place, so I pulled the needle out and did it again and my right ear had two holes. I put the ear-rings straight in – silver ones with a tear-drop pearl.

The girls in the sewing room said they couldn't keep their eyes off my ear-rings, every time I moved my head they glittered. Thelma, who worked the hem-stitching machine, wanted her ears pierced, too. She didn't have ear-rings to put in straight away, so I rubbed some white silk with vaseline and pulled it through. I told her she must twist it regularly, to stop the silk going hard from the dried blood, but she didn't and so her ears festered. I told her to bathe them every night and morning, but she wouldn't, and I had to do it for her in the lavatory at work. I wouldn't have pierced her ears if I'd known she had septic blood.

Every year, Moore's had a picnic for the staff. I bought some green and white cambric to make a divided skirt; I thought it would be ideal for climbing hills and it was the first time I ever had anything like trousers.

We went to the picnic grounds at Long Gully in buses. Before we left, Mr Charles Moore, the director, asked permission to sit beside me. He was only in his twenties and all the girls liked him. He walked round the shop familiarizing himself with everything, but I was the one he sat by.

That year there was a song, 'Oh, Charlie Take it Away', and everyone on the bus started to sing it:

> *Oh, Charlie take it away,*
> *That little bit of hair that grows upon*
> *Your upper lip, that tickles me,*
> *Charlie, take it away . . .*

I was singing with the crowd, when suddenly I saw that Mr Charles Moore was blushing, his face was as red as a lobster. He had one of those little toothbrush moustaches, and the whole bus was singing, but I shut up straight away. If he'd laughed it off, or joined in, it wouldn't have been so bad.

At Long Gully there were waitresses and long trestle tables covered with white tablecloths and when a bell was rung we sat down to everything you could think of. It was coming out of Moore's pocket, so we enjoyed it. After lunch there was a cricket match, married versus single, and then all sorts of races: old buffers', egg-and-spoon, three-legged, button-sewing race, ladies' bobbin-winding race. I went in for them all and won another walking race. I got the same prize as at the Sunday School picnic, a jar of Alpine Snow face cream. The shops only sold Alpine Snow in small jars, but both times I won a special big jar. They must have been made up for prizes.

[16]

I went to a dance at the Black Cat Dance Club and met Edmund, who had dark auburn hair with a wave. He was a decent chap and we started going out but he wouldn't take me dancing, he'd lost his last girlfriend at a dance when she went off with someone else. He often said he couldn't see me because he was going to dinner at Government House.

Edmund and his boyfriends used to hire a bus and we'd go down to the sandhills on hot nights. The girls brought the supper, the boys brought their banjos; we only sang and talked, there was no carrying on.

We went to the pictures and I liked Bebe Daniels and Lillian Gish, who was always in a sad story. Rin-Tin-Tin was the Wonder Dog, Mary Pickford took children's parts though she was a woman in her thirties, William S. Hart was in cowboy pictures (his stern face went with that sort of film). We always went upstairs to sit in the dress-circle because down below they were acting the goat.

Once a month, Moore's had a dance for the staff out on the roof garden. There was an orchestra, and the cooks in the restaurant stopped back to do fancy cooking for the supper. I made myself a lavender evening dress and beaded it in silver to match my silver shoes. I made bugle bead daisies and leaves while Edmund watched. He wouldn't take me and I wasn't going to sit there beading to go to the dance with another girl, so I asked the boy who worked in the bottle-yard to go with me. When I was dancing with him I looked up and saw he had one blue eye and one brown eye. He was a good-looking boy but I found out he had a steady girlfriend.

I wanted to go to a dance one night when Edmund was coming to see me. I was ready to leave and it was time for him to turn up, so I went into my bedroom and as I heard him knock on the front door I climbed out the window and off I went. That night Edmund asked Dad for my hand in marriage. Dad was so taken aback he couldn't answer. Mum said Edmund had better ask me as I had a mind of my own. The next night, when he did, I said I was too young. Fancy getting married at seventeen and having a mob of kids.

You went up a marble staircase to the different departments and at the top was Moore's restaurant that led out on to the roof garden, open to the sky, where there were plants in tubs, a photographer's studio and a nice view of Adelaide. Across the back of the restaurant were curtains and behind them in a space were easy-chairs, gipsy tables and a piano. At lunchtime any of the staff who played a musical instrument were allowed to go there and perform behind the curtain for the entertainment of the restaurant's customers.

I was friendly with a boy in Manchester who played the violin and a boy in Men's Wear who played the banjo. When I had my ten minutes shopping time I'd go round to see them, and ask if they'd be playing at lunchtime. If they were, I'd go there, too, and play the piano and sing. We ate our sandwiches between items.

One of the boys in the Dispatch Department started coming behind the curtain, too. He was a lively fellow, tall and dark, who drove one of Moore's vans. He didn't play anything, all he wanted was to dance with me. I never knew his real name, I called him Skeeter because everyone else did. He called me Fairy because he said I was so light on my feet.

Skeeter took me dancing at the Thistle Palais in the Caledonian Hall where there was a full jazz orchestra, and at the La Rinka Dance Class in the Blind Institution where you got fruit salad and cream for supper. One night he took me to the Pirie Street Palais, the largest ballroom in Australia with cloakrooms, retiring rooms, a buffet and a beautiful floor. I wore a red georgette dress I'd made and my silver shoes; I'd dabbed La France Rose scent behind my ears. We danced the Boronia Two-step, the Society Foxtrot and the Moonlight Waltz cheek to cheek. Skeeter gave me a kiss when we went out for a cool drink after the evening novelties were distributed – balloons, streamers, fans, trumpets, jazz sticks and mechanical mice.

It was a lucky ticket night, and I had the lucky number, but when they announced it I was still outside with Skeeter. They thought I'd gone home and gave the prize of a gold watch to someone else. Skeeter was stinking mad that I didn't get the watch. I didn't care much, because watches didn't go on my arm. I'd had gold watches and I'd had silver watches, I'd had every sort of watch, and none of them went on me; I had too much electricity in my body.

Skeeter put me on the tram home, then drove off in one of Moore's vans. But he went over a crossing when a train was coming and was killed straight out. The van was a wipe off. It was in the newspaper, but I never read the paper in the morning – the girls at work told me. He was a corker chap.

[17]

When I left Moore's in 1927, they were selling Duke and Duchess cups and saucers as souvenirs of the royal visit – I waited for hours in King William Street to see them; he looked quite nice and she had an English complexion, a snow leopard collar and a hat with two pompoms.

I'd made up my mind to work up a dressmaking business at home, I knew exactly what I wanted to do – wedding dresses, evening dresses and smart things; I didn't want to go in for the cheap stuff because anybody could run that up. But I needed experience and as there were no vacancies in Moore's sewing room upstairs, I got a job as a machinist at a place on North Terrace that did all sorts of women's clothing. The girl who sat opposite me kept putting her arm round me and touching my breasts. I didn't like it and tried to keep away from her as much as I could. She'd wait till I went to the lavatory and then she'd come, too, and she'd talk all sorts of silly things and once she kissed my cheek. She was a big girl, more plump than me. I didn't think it was right.

Dorrie started going out with Vin, who was twelve years older than her and had a house at the Bay. He was a carpenter who built boats in his spare time, in a shed at the end of his back yard. Vin's boat was the *Adel* (short for Adelaide); he moored it at the end of the jetty

53

and it had a cabin with bunks and even a lavatory. Vin took Dorrie and me sailing one weekend, but he fell in the Port River and as he swam towards the *Adel* he still had his hat on.

Vin didn't dance, he wasn't a party type, but he was a nice man, very sympathetic; if anything was wrong, he couldn't do enough for you. He was concerned about me feeling the cold. Sometimes when I went to bed and my feet were freezing, he'd pull the bedclothes up at the end and rub them till they were warm.

I made Dorrie's wedding dress out of a new sort of silky material. She wanted me to be the bridesmaid in pink lace, but there wasn't a great deal of choice among pinks; either you had the pale that was mostly used for baby's wear, or the reddy pink. I made it with a skirt that was an ordinary length in front and dipped down to a swallow tail at the back.

Dorrie wanted a square wedding cake with two tiers held up by pillars (a square cake was best for cutting, a round one wasted too many crumbs). I baked it, then iced it with hard icing over a layer of soft. I had an icing-bag with all the aluminium attachments; I did scalloping and wrote their names on top.

The wedding was on a Saturday evening. In the afternoon, Dorrie and Mum went to the football to watch Torrens play, while I decorated the house with streamers and prepared the food for the reception. When Dorrie came back from the football, she hopped in the bath and then I dressed her up. She was a heavy perspirer so I pinned a folded handkerchief inside each armhole with a gold safety-pin. She had a tulle veil with a wreath of orange blossom and carried a bouquet of daffodils – not too big, or they'd have to fiddle round putting the ring on.

Dorrie was married in a church on the Port Road. We had taxis, we had 'The Wedding March', we had toasts and musical items at the reception. I was happy, because I liked a party. Dorrie's girlfriends from the Perfection came, and Kath caught Dorrie's bouquet.

They didn't have a honeymoon, but went straight to Vin's place at the Bay in Augusta Street, the first street back from Jetty Road. Dorrie took time off from the Perfection to fix things up in the house.

After Dorrie got married, we had a spare room so Mr Briggs, an old family friend, came to board with us. His wife had died and he said it was lonely in a boarding-house; he wanted to live with a family and be part of everything that was going on.

Mr Briggs was a very clean old man who'd been born in New Zealand. He had deep blue eyes, rosy cheeks and a little tiny beard, pure white, that he kept neatly trimmed. He wore the best clothes that he could buy – he had grey suits, fawn suits and brown suits; in summer he wore a cream silk suit and a panama hat. He even had a pearl tie-pin and glacé kid shoes. Mum used to say, 'You togging yourself up again?' and Mr Briggs would answer that he was taking me out – he couldn't go out with me unless he was up to the knocker or I might drop him.

He loved to go to the pictures, but he wouldn't go on his own, so when I had a free night I'd go with him. We usually went to the Grand where they showed cowboy pictures, because they were what he liked best. He'd buy me milk kisses or chocolate cream almonds or honeymoon caramels at interval.

Mr Briggs stayed with us till he took ill and went to hospital, but he died and that was the end of him. Then his son came and took away his clothes. He'd been a kind old man, no bother at all, and we missed him.

[18]

When I started dressmaking at home, Mum used her old-fashioned sewing-machine as a deposit on a new treadle one. I made Mr Briggs' old room into a sewing room and every day I'd dust it, sweep it and mop it out. I had a clothes-horse, a long mirror, an ironing-board and an iron. Dad said he was glad I'd be keeping Mum company – I wondered whether he was worried that she might be talking to the man next door. Not Mr Lemon, but the man who looked after the horses in the bottleoh's paddock.

When the people in the neighbourhood knew I could sew, they asked how much I charged and started giving me orders. They brought their materials and cotton and I just charged them a few shillings. I got my customers by word of mouth and soon I was sewing for nearly everybody in the street. But I couldn't make quite enough money, so I worked as a machinist in a factory over the winter, when they made the summer frocks. I didn't want to make winter things, so when summer came I left. Gradually the word spread a little further, even to other suburbs, and the next winter I had enough customers to stay home.

I had a ledger book that I wrote their names and measurements in, the style they wanted and the sort of material. Wedding dresses, bridesmaids' dresses, evening dresses – it was all the same to me. I'd take the measurements and cut out on the dining-room table; I could cut out a dress without a pattern. Mum never came near me when I was cutting or measuring, but we'd talk in the sitting-room while I did hand-sewing and she crocheted. Or sometimes she'd prepare some grapes for me and I'd eat them with her in the kitchen – she'd take the skin off every grape and split it open to remove the seeds, then put the halves together again and serve them up to me on a saucer (I didn't like grapes if I had to spit out the skins and seeds).

You had to be careful with velvet – you had to see all the pile went the right way; and I'd ask Mum to hold an end while I ironed in mid-air, on the wrong side, so the pile wouldn't get flattened. Organdie and georgette were tricky; tulle and satin were very slippery and sometimes I'd pin the material on to the bed to make sure nothing moved when I cut out. I'd make flower sprays and leaves out of matching material for the evening dresses – it was nice doing work like that.

The Italian lady in the little shop opposite the Wheatsheaf Hotel had a new dress made every fortnight. She had an awful figure, but she liked everything to fit her tightly; she wanted everything smooth, to fit without a crease, and she was bulging everywhere. I made silk shirts for the chemist's son and a party frock for the butcher's daughter. I made a dress for a foreign woman and she wanted a short skirt in the Australian style, but her foreign husband controlled her and said it had to be lower – as luck had it, I'd made a big hem. Mr Warne, the railway signalman who lived round the corner, asked if I could make him an alpaca coat; he said he couldn't get any comfort out of the ones in the shops. He was a strong man from pulling the levers in the signal-box, he had plenty of muscles, and when I measured him with the tape I had to put my arms right round him. He reckoned it was the best coat he ever had and wore it till he died.

[19]

Ladies came to the house to be fitted, and afterwards they didn't want to go home. After I finished with them in the sewing-room they sat and talked to Mum in the sitting-room. When I eventually saw them out, they'd tell me I had a lovely mother. Everyone said it.

To begin with, Mum had long hair. If she undid it and sat on a chair, it touched the floor. She'd take a piece of hair and curl it round her head, do it in sections to make it flat at the back – she had to do it like that or she wouldn't have been able to get her hat on. Every now and then she snipped a bit off; she kept snipping until it came to her shoulders. She told me she'd like to have it cut shorter still, but when she asked Dad he said no. We waited a while and Mum still wanted her hair cut, so I said I'd do it (Dad couldn't say much once it was off, she couldn't put it back on again). I set it with butterfly wavers and had just combed it out when Dad came in. Tom tore out of his bedroom to see the big row start, but Dad pretended not to notice.

Mum went to the hairdresser on the Beach Road to have her hair tinted – Dad encouraged her because he was still black and she was going grey. My hair was brown with a goldy-red tinge that I supposed I got from Dad's moustache. One day when I was looking in my brother's mirror, I started singing 'Silver Threads among the Gold' – I'd found my first white hair.

If I went to the pictures with a boyfriend and it was a good show, I'd take Mum to see it, too (I never took her to anything I hadn't seen first). I paid for Mum's ticket and she liked Gary Cooper, Norma Shearer and that Swedish woman, Greta Garbo. Mum and Dad went to the pictures to see *The King of Kings*, the story of Jesus. It was a long picture that continued after interval. It was a sad story and Mum cried when they put Him on the cross.

In the hot weather, after we washed up the tea things, Mum and I often went down to Henley Beach by tram with our bathers on under our dresses. Mum thought she was too old for people to see her in her bathers, so she wouldn't go swimming while it was light; but when it was dark she'd swim right out to the end of the jetty. I didn't like it, because every now and then there were sharks.

Mum was always in her fern house – she had maiden-hair fern, bridesmaid's fern, sword fern; and fuchsias and wax flowers in hanging baskets. Dad was very fond of carnations, so Mum grew some beauties – great big pink ones for him to put in his buttonhole.

I was a great shifter. Nobody knew from one week to the next where they were going to sleep, because I'd shift them out of one room and into another. Dad said he didn't dare go into a room without putting the light on; if he tried to get into bed in the dark he might miss it. I slept in every room of the house, the front verandah and the back one. One night in a heatwave I put my bed on the back verandah; early in the morning Gwen, the youngest Lemon girl next door, came over as it was too hot to sleep inside. She hopped in with me and then went home to breakfast.

Gwen and I went for a holiday to Port Noarlunga. We rented two rooms of a cottage called Coo-ee and every day we walked over the sandhills and out on the reef. One day a school of sharks came in on the inside of the reef, and all the fish were frightened into the shallows. Big fish were jumping out of the water and lots of people were down there grabbing them. I grabbed one and put it on the sand, then I grabbed another. Two big fish were too much for Gwen and me, but on the way back to

Coo-ee I saw my brother on his motorbike so he took one of the fish home, even though he wouldn't eat any of it. He reckoned it was cruel to eat fish, he wouldn't even eat poultry.

Tom's bike was a Harley Davidson, and I often went with him to watch the motorbike races in the sandhills. The bikes had chains round their back wheels to give more grip in the sand. Some of them turned over, but their riders were never hurt because they jumped off just in time. In hot weather, after Tom came home from work, he'd give Dad a ride down to Henley to have a swim before tea.

Whenever Tom had a new suit made I had to alter the waistcoat. He was broad-chested and waistcoats buttoned high, but he didn't like to ask the tailor to cut his down. If he wanted new shoes or shirts or anything, he wouldn't choose them himself. He'd give me a ride on his motorbike to one of the big stores in town and I'd have to buy them for him. He said I knew exactly what he needed.

Dad gave Mum a wireless in a rosewood cabinet, and she'd sit and crochet tablecloths and doilies every night, and listen right through till the GPO chimes, the National Anthem and close down (Dad put a mat in front of the wireless and he'd lie there and listen to the news, nothing else, then go back to his reading). Sometimes when Dad went to town he bought chocolates for me and great big jujubes for Mum – she said you mightn't get much for your money, but they were what she liked. If I saw a small pipe, I'd buy it and Dad would be as pleased as Punch when I gave it to him for his birthday. When Tom's firm sent him to Melbourne, he wrote and asked Mum what she'd like him to bring back, but Mum said she couldn't ask him to bring back anything. So I wrote the letter for her and told Tom that Mum could do with a new brush and comb and mirror set for her dressing-table, and that I'd like a gold bangle, one that fitted up your arm and was worn with a fancy lace handkerchief tucked through it. They were fashionable and I thought I might as well have one. Tom had the money.

Mum and Dorrie arranged a surprise party for my twenty-first birthday. Hazel had invited me over to her place that afternoon, but when I got there she was all dolled up and ready to go out. We talked for a while and then I started home – I thought it was darned funny, because I hadn't expected to go home to tea; usually, if I went to Hazel's, I had tea there. I walked back slowly, there didn't seem anything to rush for. They must have worked like mad while I was out, because when I came in, the house was decorated with streamers and was full of people. Mum had made the birthday cake, but she'd sent it out to be iced in pink and silver; there were silver cachous on it and twenty-one candles. Dorrie gave me a Star of Bethlehem brooch, Tom gave me a cut-glass fruit bowl. Mum and Dad's present was a set of blue jersey-silk underwear.

On Saturdays when I went down the Bay to see Dorrie, we'd always go window-shopping along Jetty

Road. One Saturday I saw a hat in La Mode's window that just looked like Mum. It was a light navy, a fine silky straw, with a little bunch of fuchsias at the side. I knew it would suit Mum; I'd made her a navy dress and it was exactly the same colour. I brought the hat home and told Mum it was to be her Christmas box, but she could try it on to see if she liked it. It suited her down to the ground, she looked really smart. The hat went back in its bag and I said it was going right on top of the Christmas tree.

That Christmas, a pine tree had come up in the bottleoh's paddock. It was the right size for a Christmas tree, so one evening when it was nearly dark, I hopped over the fence and sawed it off. Dorrie and Vin came for Christmas dinner with the forelady from the Perfection. I had presents for everybody and I'd put them all on the tree and decorated it with candles, tinsel and little glass balls. Dad had killed one of our white muscovy-ducks and Mum cooked it for dinner; she'd made two Christmas puddings and I'd made two Christmas cakes – we kept one pudding and one cake for New Year's.

After dinner, we went into the sitting-room and I was the one to call out the names on the presents. I gave Mum her hat first. Then Dad played his piano-accordion, he could play anything we wanted to sing.

[20]

The Depression was bad – girls didn't want wedding dresses and I lowered the price of my dressmaking to keep my customers. Dad and Tom still had their jobs, but there were only two other men in our street who were working. Mr Lemon worked for the Council and Mr Prisk, who couldn't make a living from cabinetmaking any more, took an empty shop in George Street and mended boots. Men came round selling all sorts of odds and ends – moth-balls, needles, jelly powders, corn cures; Mum always bought something, she was sorry for anybody out of work because Dad and Tom were bringing home money and we were all right. She knitted booties and sewed rompers for the newspaper's contest to clothe the babies of the poor; she sent in cakes and puddings to the Christmas appeal for the needy; she bought a joint of meat for a widow up the street with four children.

Tom met Louisa when he was putting in the sprinkler system at the chemical factory where she worked. None of us liked her, but we didn't show it. She was passable, but nothing out of the box; she was a funny type who wanted everybody to make a fuss of her all the time, but she didn't invite any of her family to the wedding. I didn't want my brother to marry her, but I didn't say anything, it was nothing to do with me. It was his choice, he had to put up with her. I sewed their curtains and cushions, altered Tom's wedding waistcoat and made the white satin wedding dress that had a train with a frill and tight-fitting sleeves with a row of buttons and loops, right up to the elbow, so Louisa could get her hands out. I was the bridesmaid in pink French crêpe (Louisa wouldn't have her sister, she said she was too old fashioned). I made it with a flared skirt and a cowl neckline that had diamanté clasps on either side.

After they were married in Holy Trinity (the wedding photos came out all right, except that Louisa held her sheath of white gladiolis up too high), they went to live in a new bungalow that was the admiration of all their friends. Mum and Dad gave them a deep pink eiderdown and they had a walnut bedroom suite, a kitchen cabinet with cathedral glass doors, and easy chairs covered in Genoa velvet.

Louisa didn't care for married life, though she'd been breaking her neck to get married. My brother told me he wasn't over-sexed and could go for three months before he wanted it, but she got caught fairly quick. When she found out she was pregnant she was upset; Tom couldn't get any sense out of her and asked me to go down and see her. I rushed in and threw my arms round her (but I never did like her) and pretended I was pleased about the baby. I said we'd have to start making baby's clothes and made such a fuss of her that she got excited. She was seven months pregnant when she caught her heel in the platform of the tram, as she was getting off at the Wheatsheaf Hotel. A man standing by the pub tried to catch her, but she fell on her stomach.

65

That night the baby started coming so Tom had to ring for an ambulance.

Violet was a very small baby with the marks of the forceps on her forehead. Tom had to stay home and look after her on Saturday nights when Louisa went dancing. One night she came home with a man and Tom got so mad he tore all her evening dresses into strips.

[21]

'Your father hasn't touched me for four years,' Mum suddenly said to me at tea one night, and then Dad said, 'Well, I don't expect to wear myself out.' I didn't say anything, I supposed it was just something she needed to say. But he loved her, and whenever he came home he put his arms round her, even if she was sitting down crocheting.

Mum was dying for me to get married and have a baby (she said if I ever got into trouble, she'd bring the baby up as if it was her own), but I'd made up my mind when I was sixteen that I wasn't going to do either and I stuck to it. I was very independent and always had my say and did what I wanted. When I saw what was happening to my brother's marriage, I was glad I'd made up my mind so early.

I went out with a lot of boyfriends. I didn't love them or want to get married or anything, we were just good pals, but I had several proposals. And one day a big flabby man, who lived round the corner next to the priest's house, stopped me in the street and asked me to marry him. He said, 'You're one of us, aren't you?' – he meant was I a Catholic. When I said I wasn't, he took his proposal back.

Once a man came out of some bushes when I was walking home late at night and started wobbling his thing at me, so I ran. He couldn't chase me, he had his pants down.

Some new people came to live across the road and they turned their fruit garden into a tennis-court and had tennis matches on Saturday afternoons. I didn't belong to the club, but they'd invite me over and one Saturday I met a man who lived over the other side of town. We didn't meet again, but he wrote about half a dozen pages to me every week and I wrote the same to him, sometimes more. I had a whole caseful of his letters (not love letters, but friendship letters) and he must have watched me, because he knew everywhere I went.

Hazel's brother, Eric, was one man that I really liked, but he had a habit of calling me Goldy because I had gold fillings in my front teeth. I hated being called that, so I went and had them all out and got false ones. We went dancing together and made up a snake dance. I was the snake trying to entice him and we never touched. It was like Salome's dance, but it wasn't the Dance of the Seven Veils. When we did it, everyone stopped dancing to watch.

Eric had a very bad accident on his motorbike and

one leg had to be cut off. He opened a shop, but serving behind the counter was too much for him. Though I wasn't in love with Eric, I might have married him for pity's sake. In the mornings he could have been in the shop, fresh from bed; he could have had mid-day dinner and then I could have gone in the shop in the afternoon and he could have rested. But he never asked me – he said he'd never marry. I wondered if he'd been affected down below in any way, he could have been damaged.

When I met Audrey again she was married, but she was highly sexed and had a boyfriend because her husband wasn't satisfying her enough. The last time I'd seen her, she'd sung a Scots song out the front at a concert before she left the Thebarton School. She'd gone to the Methodist Ladies' College, she was a débutante who had her photo taken by Rembrandt and then she'd gone to the School of Arts and Crafts where she'd done Historic Ornament. Now she did china painting and had an overfed bulldog.

Audrey was striking and men fell for her. She had plenty of money because her father had died and left her well off – she had fur coats, lovely dresses, a cream car and two bedrooms. I often went to dances with Audrey and her boyfriend and sometimes we went to the Empire Theatre to watch the boxing, but we never saw any blood. Audrey bought all her boyfriend's clothes and dressed him exactly like her husband. If you saw Audrey and her boyfriend walking down the street, you didn't know whether it was her husband or not.

Audrey invited me and some of her other girlfriends to meet the Lady Mayoress and I brought a walnut cake for afternoon tea. The Lady Mayoress tested our etiquette by asking each of us in turn what we'd do if a cup of tea was brought to us and it had spilled in the saucer. I was the only one who gave the right answer, even though the others were college girls.

[22]

I was a lady's companion, once – to a rich dame down the Bay. Mrs Snowball's husband had died and she was lonely (she'd buried him just before I came). She had plenty of money and a nice home with the portraits of eight generations of Snowballs on the dining-room walls. She was a timid sort of woman who was fat because her thyroid gland had lost power. She never had any children because she married late, after her father died – he'd said that if she married without his consent he'd disinherit her.

I lived with her, but went home to see Mum and Dad every weekend. I was her companion in every way. If anyone came to the door I had to help her entertain them, I had to see that the cleaning lady didn't damage the Family Bible when she dusted it. Every morning, after Mrs Snowball had her breakfast, we'd sit in the small sitting-room where there was a fire and I'd do her hair in different styles and she loved it.

One of the bedrooms that was never used was full of trunks and Mrs Snowball opened them and showed me the clothes she'd worn as a girl. The hats were piled up with flowers and all kinds of creeping plants and grasses. The dresses had baby-ribbon, zigzag frills and leg-of-mutton sleeves. There were parasols and an ostrich-feather fan. Mrs Snowball said that when she was a girl and didn't have any colour, she'd sleep at night with slices of raw beefsteak tied on each cheek.

After that, whenever Mrs Snowball went out, I'd dress up in her old-fashioned clothes and parade in front of the mirror, but I was always frightened she'd come home before I got them off.

Mrs Snowball's brother, the ear, nose and throat specialist from Queensland, came to stay. He was an older man, but we got on very well and he took me to the Amusement Park by the beach, where we explored the far places of the earth in the shadowy labyrinths of the River Caves – one minute it was Hawaii with flame trees and lagoons, then Venice with gondola posts reflected across the water, then a foggy corner of London.

Mrs Snowball became paralysed and couldn't talk or get up or anything, so her niece, May, came to help me. When we made the bed, we'd just lift her and roll her over. When we washed her and cleaned her up, May did the dirty end and I did the top end.

There was a piano in the room opposite Mrs Snowball's bedroom and I'd play it and sing to her. She'd cock her ear – she couldn't lift her head, but she could cock her ear round to listen to all that was going on.

I knew she'd liked toffee when she was well, so I made her some. I told her to suck it, not swallow it, and I sat there all the time, just in case, because if she did I'd have to yank it out. I knew she loved the colour lavender, so I'd plait her hair and tie it with lavender ribbon – she could just see the bows on her shoulders.

When May found Mrs Snowball dead after lunch one day, she went hysterical. I had to take her by the shoulders and almost shake her head off before she stopped howling.

[23]

I was a pink bridesmaid for the third time when Bessie Warne, the signalman's daughter, got married. Warnes weren't well off, so I made her wedding dress for nothing, and from the satin that was over I made her a lucky horseshoe. The bridegroom paid for my material as his present and I chose taffeta because it wasn't too expensive; I made it with a long bodice and a gathered skirt so I could wear it for an evening dress later. But I was tired of pink, I would've liked blue or light green or a nice shade of yellow. The bridegroom had an orange tree in his garden and brought over a bunch of blossom on the wedding morning so I could make a wreath for Bessie's hair – it had to be done at the last minute so the flowers wouldn't droop. And I put orange blossom on her lucky horseshoe.

The Warnes' son, Bob, had been courting a girl who lived on a farm near Port Lincoln, on the West Coast. She had her wedding dress already, but asked me to make her tulle veil and mittens and the flower-girls' dresses. She sent over their measurements and I did what I could at home, and was invited over to the Coast to finish things off.

Mum was crying as she waved me off on the ship to Port Lincoln. I shared a cabin with the only other woman passenger and she had the bottom bunk, I had the top one. There were a lot of soldiers on board, going off to camp and the two of us got all the attention – the other woman played the piano and they took it in turns to dance with me. Whenever I put my glass down, one of them would fill it up with beer; I didn't drink beer, only lemonade, so I'd tip it into a potted palm in a corner, but then they'd see my glass was empty and fill it up again (they must have thought I was a real drinker). It was very rough during the night and the stewardess said in the morning that I was the only one to want a cup of tea, all the others were being sick.

When we reached Port Lincoln, I went to a restaurant for breakfast and a commercial traveller came and sat at my table. I had to catch the afternoon train to the town where Bob Warne was going to meet me and the traveller said he'd drive me to the station to make my booking, then take me to all the places he was going to do business, and we could have a talk in between calls. He told me about living up North and betting with dingo scalps and eagle-hawk claws when there was a race-meeting. But he was a married man and when he drove me back to the station I said goodbye and never saw him again.

Bob Warne was full of devilment. He put a walking-stick with a face-washer round it in my bed and waited for me to yell like murder, thinking it was a snake – but I didn't, because I always folded my bedclothes back before I got in. When I went down to tell him off he threw a bucket of water over me; in the morning he pinched my wet pyjamas off the clothes-line and hung them over the cow-yard gate. The next night when Bob sat beside me on the wall of the fishpond, I pushed him in the water, then went for my life.

There was no church near by, so the wedding service was to be held in a hall that we decorated with paper chains and streamers. Bob kept suggesting I should climb the ladder to hang up the Chinese lanterns – he wanted to see up my wide-leg scanties.

Being a country wedding, everybody came from miles around. We all wore our evening clothes for the service, because we'd be dancing afterwards.

Bob and his bride had arranged to spend their wedding night in a hut in the bush, but it was one of the hottest nights ever known in Australia and there was a bushfire.

On the ship back to Adelaide, I was looking for the lavatory and put my hand on a door to steady myself. It wasn't locked and I fell into a cabin where Bob and his bride were sitting on a bunk. They were on their honeymoon so I couldn't get out quick enough.

The Second World War started and I had a letter from the Authorities to say I wasn't allowed to stop home and sew. I had to work at something to do with the War, so I applied for a job at Holdens, where I knew they did military sewing. I got it and came home with a button that had my number on it. Tom kicked up a fuss, he said Holdens wasn't a fit place for me to go, he reckoned it had a bad name because all the larrikins worked there.

First of all I was down on the benches counting out pieces of material to be sewn, but I used to pass out from the fumes of the paint shop near by so Mr Bott, the manager, put me on an electric sewing-machine, sewing haversacks. You had to do a hundred in an hour; at first I couldn't, but I did eventually and even had time to spare, so I kept going down to have a talk to the lady who made the tea in the dining-room.

We'd tell one another what we'd done before we'd come to Holdens. Most of the others had been typists and shop girls and when I said I'd been a dressmaker, one girl asked me to make her wedding dress. She wanted sequins on the bodice and a Russian head-dress of satin with sequins all over it. It took a long time because I did it at night. I didn't charge her anything, I said she could have it for a wedding present.

But I didn't like sewing haversacks. I'd been used to dainty things, not hard old khaki canvas. One lunch-time I was talking to a man down the other end of the factory; he said they were starting up a new type of work to do with aircraft and wanted to train somebody to teach the girls. So every lunch hour after that, they trained me on aircraft work, until I was ready to give my notice to Mr Bott.

I went to night school to learn how to manage people, and wore a grey coat to show that I was a leading hand with full authority over a hundred-and-twenty girls. There were five blind men (I had to take their hands and show them what I wanted done) and five women who were deaf and dumb. I'd learnt finger spelling from a deaf and dumb alphabet printed on the back of my dictation book at school, but they soon taught me some of the sign language which was much quicker.

I had to teach everyone how to do the de-burring on the aluminium aircraft parts. All the roughness had to be taken off with a sharp knife; there were little parts and big parts and they all had numbers, not names. It was very rough work for the girls; they were supplied with gloves but soon wore them out, so I asked Cyril, the assistant manager, for sticking-plaster to wrap round their fingers. Some of the jobs were terribly fiddly so I'd give half a dozen to each girl out of the tray – if I'd given a whole tray to one girl, all her fingers would have been bleeding. The tops of my fingers had bled when I was learning, and Mum had worried when I came home with sticking-plaster wrapped round them.

One blind man wanted standing-up jobs, so he used to do the aircraft wings on a great big bench. When we had air-raid practice, I had to see that all my girls and blind men and deaf mutes got out and were sheltered. Then I had to go back to make quite sure no one was left; I thought that if they bombed the place, I'd be the only one to go up in smoke.

Every pay-day I went round the departments with a tin, collecting money for the soldiers. They had a Queen competition to raise money for the War effort, too; our department had the White Queen, the two other departments had a Red and a Blue Queen. The three Queens were sent to one of the shops in the city to pick out their material and have an evening dress made up any way they liked. Our Queen was going to be married, so it was lucky she was the White Queen (she picked out the best material she could buy and had it made for a wedding dress). Anyone could help to raise money for the Queen, so when I came home at night I made sponge cakes and a girl whose father had cows for his milk-round gave me a big jar of cream (they weren't allowed to sell cream during the War, it had to be made into butter or cheese). I piped the cream into scrolls on the sponges, then decorated them with cherries or strawberries or pineapple pieces, then sprinkled on coconut. I only made three sponges a night, but I made them all double. We cut them into pieces and sold them, and the White Queen was the Queen of Queens at the ball in the Palais because she raised the most money.

At Christmas we had a party. We knocked off at lunchtime and were allowed as long as we liked. I sent the bosses an invitation, but they refused because they had their own party. I'd rung up the caterers at Port

Adelaide and asked the girls to bring in white single sheets (with their names on them in ink) to cover the tables. There was a paper cap and a bonbon beside everyone's plate and we had pies and pasties, sausage rolls and sandwiches, and every kind of cake you could think of; and there were fruit salads, jellies and trifles – we had tons to eat. Girls brought their musical instruments and I made a speech through the microphone. The Christmas cake was cut and a piece rolled up in everyone's serviette so they could take it home.

[25]

A man on a bike came round the corner going like mad and knocked Mum down while she was crossing George Street. She walked home, but wouldn't go to the doctor. Then Mum stood on the edge of the sofa in her bedroom to dust the top of the wardrobe. The sofa tipped up and hit her in the side with its back; she broke a rib in two places but still cooked the tea. It was the same place where the man on the bike had hit her, but she wouldn't go to the hospital to be X-rayed and the only doctor we could find was drunk. He said he wasn't capable of bandaging Mum up, so I had to do it. I tore a wide strip off a roll of calico Mum kept for making pillow-slips and sheets; I bound her up and laced her into an old pair of stays (when her side healed up we used the bandage to make pillow-slips, as it wasn't stained with blood).

But she kept complaining of a pain in her side and was always lying down on the sofa. She wouldn't give in, she kept going, she went on like that for twelve months and then one Sunday when she was cooking midday dinner she turned to me and said she was finished, I could please myself what I did with her. I got a taxi and took her to the hospital where she stayed for a week. The doctors said a lump had formed inside her; she'd left it too long and there was nothing they could do. They sent her home and she took to her bed.

Dad had retired, so he looked after her in the daytime and when I came home at night I washed and fed her. She was a very poor eater; I'd make her a scrambled egg and light milky things for dessert, but she'd only eat a few spoonfuls. She still liked her cup of tea – I'd wait till it was cool and then lift it to her lips. The first time I went to wash her, she kept her eyes on me all the time but never said a word. I took off her nightgown and washed her face and arms and legs – I felt embarrassed and knew she did, too, so then I took the sheet and threw it over her face and went straight ahead and washed her up top and down below.

She wasn't interested any more in anything, she was going downhill. All her nighties were silk with low necks and short sleeves, and you couldn't bury her like that. I had some madapollam that was fine enough for handkerchiefs so I made her up a gown – but very roughly, because I was expecting her to go and you can't dress them once they've stiffened. It had long sleeves and lace round the neck, and I made it look as nice as I could. I pressed it and hung it over the end of the bed and then she held out her hands. I thought she wanted me to take her in my arms, but she was feeling hot and wanted me to scent her, so I sponged her with eau-de-cologne. Then I touched her forehead to feel her temperature and her face fell into my hands and I called to Dad that she was gone.

I never knew anyone to ask and, anyhow, I thought Mum would rather I did it – I'd never laid anyone out before but I just seemed to know what to do (I often thought I must have inherited something from my French grandmother who was a doctor). I washed her and put her new gown on and did her hair (I didn't put any powder on her because she wasn't going anywhere). I took her wedding ring off and her teeth out to clean, then put them back. I put cottonwool up her nose and two florins on her eyes to keep them closed (I didn't like half-closed eyes); her mouth had fallen open so I bound up her jaw in one of Dad's scarves. I didn't have any cotton stockings so I put on the pink bed-socks, sent years ago from South Africa, that she'd never worn. Then I took the pillows away so she lay flat, and pushed her over on her side so I could get the top of the ironing-board under her to keep her straight while her body stiffened. I crossed her hands on her chest so she'd fit into the coffin, put a towel between her legs, just in case, then pulled the sheet up over her because it seemed best.

The coffin was lined with white satin, dented in with

pins; the undertaker came in the morning and put it on a trestle in the sitting-room. He covered Mum with scallopy net, so all you could see were her face and hands. The florist kept coming with wreaths (even the Salvation Army sent one) and people brought bouquets from their gardens, so there were flowers all round her.

She was buried on Christmas Eve, in West Terrace Cemetery, a month after her sixtieth birthday. It was a nice funeral, lots of people went and a minister talked at the grave. Mum was put down deep to leave room for Dad on top.

[26]

When Dad said he hadn't noticed me doing any crying over Mum, I said not everyone wore their heart on their sleeve. I was always thinking of her; one day I saw a pot-plant in the florist's window and thought it was just what she'd like – it was only while I was waiting to be served that I realized Mum wasn't there any more, so I walked out of the shop. We'd been so close that people had said we were like sisters but I didn't cry till three months after she died, and then it came in a flood. It happened when I had a pain with my period, and put my foot on the rung of the chair by the stove to ease it – and I remembered it was something Mum had done when her side was worrying her.

Dad always wore a tie and a waistcoat with his watch-chain across it; he pottered round in the shed, making things with his lathe, and he made me a dustpan but it was too heavy to use. A friend he'd worked with in engineering visited him every week for a talk; he was a tall man, very military looking, who'd been in the Indian Army. And Dad read books about things that were important (he never read novels); he often looked at his collection of stamps – old ones, dating right back to before I was born; he wrote letters to South Africa and listened to the wireless. I'd think of little jobs for Dad to do to keep him occupied. He emptied the water from the ice-chest and collected the hens' eggs and bought the bread. I'd tell him to go round to the butcher and get the meat for the cats and cut it up and feed them (but I never let him buy the meat we ate, because they might pass him off with the tough stuff). He fed the fowls with bran and pollard in the morning, with wheat at night, and I told him to pick a few of the outside leaves of the silverbeet every day and tie them to a post in the fowl house.

Dad didn't have wrinkles and his hair stayed black with just one or two grey hairs (he never went white or bald); he still dyed his moustache but he had a hernia that used to come out, and he'd have to sit on the couch and gradually push it back in.

The War went on, and the Japs got down as far as Darwin and did a bit of bombing. We had blackout curtains and ration tickets, and if you had a pair of nylon stockings you'd been out with a Yank or you'd done something you shouldn't have to get them. Peanuts were short, they only let nursing mothers have

81

them. There was a girl at Holdens who always sat with her overcoat on and we couldn't make out why – till she got bigger and stopped home and had her baby.

One of the managers was always hanging round, whispering in my ear. The girls used to ask me when it was on and I'd say it was nothing like that at all. One day he came up and started telling me about his parties and changing partners. Then he asked me what night my father went out and I said he never did. Some of them got the huffs when you passed them up – as if I'd have taken on a married man.

The doctor told me one day that Dad hadn't long to live; he loved the ocean and wanted some sea air, so I packed his bag and off he went to stay with Dorrie and Vin at the Bay. He had the front bedroom, the lavender room, where Dorrie and Vin had slept when they were first married – there was a lavender bedspread and curtains, I'd made the lavender silk light-shade with its bead fringe; the cream lino was patterned with little lavender flowers and there was a wool rug hooked into a lavender sunken garden.

I went to the Bay every weekend and could see Dad's health was going down. He was very white, the way sick people get; he seemed to be fading and took to his bed. Dad had been a man who didn't like anyone to see what he was doing, but now he just kicked off his pyjama pants when we put him on the commode – he went childish and the district nurse came to help Dorrie.

One Saturday morning when I got there, Dorrie told

me he'd died in the night. The district nurse had fixed him up and laid him out. While we were waiting for the undertaker to come, Vin got a bit hostile and said, 'You better get him off my bed.'

Dad had been a man who kept himself to himself and to his home, so there were only a few family wreaths. We went back to the Bay after the funeral and everyone got a shock when the will was read because the house had been left to me. Dorrie flared up and said she'd contest it (but she never did); she thought the house should have been divided between us and I should have gone to live with her and Vin.

I gave Dad's suits to the Salvation Army; Tom took his shirts and jumpers, his shoes and socks (I kept a couple of woollen pairs for bed-socks), but he didn't want his underclothes because Dad had worn long underpants and flannels. And Tom took Dad's tools and some of the machinery in the shed and the framed photo of Mum in her lace blouse and pearls. Dad's Indian Army friend asked if he could have something as a memento. He was getting to be an old man himself, so I thought of Dad's ebony walking-stick with the silver knob – if he got a bit wobbly in his dotage he'd have a stick.

I missed Dad a lot. I was all right at work where I had plenty to do and there were other people to take my mind off things. But as soon as I got in the front door, I'd lean against it and the tears would flow. It went on like that for a while and then the girl who was my inspector at Holdens said she thought I ought to stay with her and her cousin for a while, instead of being home on my own.

The cousin was a clairvoyant. She told me something was going to happen at Holdens, and I was going to be very quick and prevent somebody from getting badly hurt. A few days later when I was walking through the department I heard a yell from a girl on one of the machines. I raced over and switched off the power, but the machine had pulled most of the hair out of one side of her head. She was stuck in the machine and while she screamed I got the big shears to cut away the hair that was caught. I took her to the Casualty and she was lucky, because she could have been scalped.

[27]

When I went back to the house in Pearl Street, I couldn't see the bottom of the yard for weeds, they were higher than my head. It was summer and they were drying out so I scattered newspaper here, there and everywhere and put a match to it: up in the air she went and down she came, all ash. The rosemary hedge went up in smoke by mistake but the fire must have killed most of the pests in the yard, because I didn't see any snails or insects for ages.

I was great on growing from slips. If I happened to be out walking in the street and saw a plant I liked hanging over a fence, I'd nip a piece off. I grew a pink hibiscus by the shed and a fuchsia by the side fence; I even grew

84

climbing roses from slip – I had a Lorraine Lee and one of those tiny little threepenny-bit roses, people used to go mad on them for shoulder sprays with silver-paper stems. My sweetpeas were all the colours you could think of and if you went out in the yard all you could smell was their perfume, there were so many of them; first thing in the morning it just about took your breath away.

Some rhubarb was pale, mine was a beautiful red right through and I grew carrots, beetroot, parsnips, potatoes, tomatoes, silverbeet, sugar cabbages and along the edge of the vegetable garden I grew sweetcorn. I bought a pumpkin and kept the seeds and planted some by the fowl house door; I trained them so they went up, and I had a fair crowd of flowers and then pumpkins all over the fowl house roof – they were so big I had to get my brother to lift them down. There was a passion-fruit vine along the bottleoh's fence; I grew a lemon tree and even a fig tree from a seed.

A friend on the Beach Road gave me a couple of bantams because she knew I loved birds, and I christened them Darby and Joan. They were a gingery colour with light fawny feathers down their legs like a fan and wherever the little hen went, the little rooster went, too; if she sat down to lay an egg, he sat down beside her in the nest and when she came out, he came out and if he thought she wanted some food, he'd go and get it for her. The big black Orpington rooster was trying to carry on with the little hen, so I put Darby and Joan in a separate compartment in the fowl house – but it was too late because the old rooster had done his job already. Joan laid four eggs, slightly bigger than usual; she sat on them with Darby beside her and four chickens, slightly bigger than bantams, came out – a black one, a deep creamy one, a buff one, a black and white speckly one.

Jinny was a big fowl, a Rhode Island red, with a peculiar curved beak, a humped ginger body and long legs. She was quite old and had never laid an egg, but suddenly she laid one under the apple tree that grew up through the fowl house; she sat on the egg under the tree till it hatched. It was the dead spit of her, so I called it Jinny's Girl.

Caw-caw was a white fowl and one night I came home from Holdens to find she'd caught her foot in the wire of the fowl house. She'd been pulling and pulling, one of her claws was nearly torn off, so after I unhooked it I put her in the shed on a bag. Every morning I'd feed and water her, bathe her foot and bandage it up; then, when I came home at night I'd do the same thing again. I didn't put her back in the fowl house till it was thoroughly better and after that, as soon as she saw me coming, she'd run up and hold out her foot and cry, 'Caw-caw, Caw-caw'.

The big black rooster didn't have a name, but I gave him a good hiding once. He had spurs on his legs and he came trotting up and was going to spur me, so I got hold of him round the neck and slapped his face both sides, to show him I was boss. He was as good as gold after that.

My fowls loved me and I loved them. I gave them shell-grit to make shells for their eggs and regularly whitewashed the part of the fowl house where they slept. When I raked it out I'd sprinkle the droppings over the garden and dig them in, they were better than any other manure. Sometimes I'd sit on a box in the fowl house and sing quietly. Jinny and Caw-caw sat on my knees and if I stroked one, the other would be jealous. I sang 'Bonny Black Bess' and 'I Belong to Glasgow' while the fowls sat round me; but the black rooster would strut about crowing, so I'd tell him to shut up and sit down. When I sang to them, they laid in the night as well as the day, though some of the night-time eggs had very thin shells.

I had a lot of eggs but I wasn't very fond of them and rarely ate one. I gave most of them away to people in the street, and when Dorrie and Tom came I'd give them a bagful. I tried to kill a fowl once – I tied her legs up and put her head on the chop-block and got the axe but I couldn't do it, every time I went to hit her she looked at me. In the end I told her to go back to the fowl house.

[28]

Miss Evans at Holdens thought she was somebody, but her job was to supervise the ladies' lavatories to make sure no one stayed there too long. She was an older woman who thought she had her niceties about her, but she didn't like me (I didn't ask her to help with the flowers for our Christmas party and she wasn't invited because she never ate her lunch in our dining-room). It was against the rules for me to go to the lavatory with another person and when she told Cyril, the assistant manager, that I went with the girl who was my inspector, I knew she had it in for me. Cyril had it in for me, too, and believed Miss Evans, even though I said she was telling lies. He wanted to shift me to another department so I rang up the Co-op where they handled dairy produce for the troops, to ask if there were any vacancies. I went to see the manager of the Butter Department with my credentials and we had a talk as if we were real cobbers and then he asked me to start the next Monday.

There were departments for Eggs, Butter, Milk and Cheese. Eggs was up the front, then you went down a passage to Butter. I spent the first week outside the butter room, where the butter boxes were kept. It was Taffy and Old Ted's job to repair the boxes and then another girl and I had to clean them out with a little hand-brush, then line them with white paper. Taffy and Old Ted wore carpenter's aprons and worked at separate benches. Taffy was always whistling or singing; he was a very helpful man, nice to talk to, but Old Ted was always trying to smooch round me. He'd come up quietly behind me, then stand close and talk very low; I'd keep moving back to get a butter box between us.

You could have a good old chat while you worked, but the other girl was bad tempered because she worked at night as an usherette in a picture theatre, as well as working at the Co-op all day. She usually came in late and one day when I said good morning she must have thought I was being sarcastic, because she pushed me in one of the boxes. They were big square boxes and when Taffy helped me out I knew I'd hurt my back, so I got her up against the bench and took hold of her hair and slapped her face till I was tired – it was pretty red when I finished.

Then I was moved to the butter room where the butter was made in two big churns that nearly went up to the ceiling. Eventually it passed along a conveyor belt and a knife came down and chopped it into pounds; two mechanical hands picked each pound up and put it on a wrapper, then a machine folded the wrapper and the pounds came to me to be weighed. It didn't matter if they were overweight, but if one was under, a girl had to open up the wrapper and plonk on a bit more butter. You had to be quick because the pounds kept coming, and then my two packers put them into boxes that went into the freezing chambers (we were producing all the butter for the troops and for the people of South Australia).

It was a nice place to work after Holdens, where I'd been on my feet all day. At the Co-op, I had a high stool to sit on and I got one of the men to put a little cupboard up for my cup, my jar of sugar, my tea and teapot. I could buy my milk cheaply, and when I wanted butter I just took a wrapper and grabbed some out of the big churn. At lunchtime I didn't go up to the dining-room, but sat round in a circle with the girls outside the butter room. Sometimes I'd go down to the engine room to see a chap I was friendly with; one day his wife was there, I supposed she was wondering if I was going to take her husband from her.

There were about twenty cats at the Co-op, roaming all over the place to keep the mice down. One pregnant half-Persian used to come up and sit begging while I had my lunch. She liked cake, so I brought two slices – one for her and one for me. The woman who stamped the cheeses lined out an old butter box with paper and the cat had her kittens in it. The biggest of the batch, and the only boy, was saved for me and I called him Mickey. I peeped at him every day and took him home before I really should have, because everybody was after him.

Mickey was a grey kitten with white paws and a biscuit-coloured stomach and when he was four months old I took him back to the Co-op to be doctored by Les, who worked in the machine shop. He grew into a big cat, solid as a rock, who could jump high off the ground and smack a tennis-ball with his paw when I bounced it against the wall. Mrs Turner, across the road, had some white angora rabbits that ran round her garden and Mickey brought the mother rabbit home and put her on the back door mat, then brought her babies over one at a time. Mickey slept under the fuchsia bush and I brushed him every day because he didn't like to be washed. He was a very loving cat, who seemed to understand everything I said. Sometimes in winter, I'd sit out in the garden in my warm coat and he'd come and sit beside me; I'd tell him I was awfully cold round the shoulders and he'd jump up and curl round my neck. He went into the fowl house and never touched the fowls, but he was fond of their bran and pollard. I fed him on stewing steak and he liked ice-cream. But feeding him ice-cream was expensive, so I bought ice-blocks instead and Mickey didn't know the difference. I'd put the ice-block on the front verandah and it would slip down to one end as he licked it, then he'd turn round and lick it back the other way.

[29]

I got myself in with the girls at the Co-op, they all seemed to like me. I took them in lettuces from my garden and gave a different girl a bunch of sweetpeas every morning – even the conductor of the tram I caught wanted a bunch for his invalid wife. The girls sometimes came home and had dinner with me after work, and if it was a hot night they'd take it in turns to have a shower while I cooked the roast. I'd set the table and make the dessert and cream sponges the night before, and we used Mum's good linen serviettes from South Africa. A week before Christmas we'd have a special Christmas dinner and I'd have a tree with a present under it for every one of them.

Mabel worked in the Egg Department and had to

hold eggs under a powerful electric light and those with green yolks, blood spots or worms were passed aside; she was a lot younger than me, but we got on very well together. She was a wiry type with permed hair, full of life, though she was thin and always said she felt cold. She didn't wear brassieres as she didn't have much to put in them, so I said to put a pair on because without them she was all loose and the wind got into her lungs.

We wore white overalls at the Co-op, and I knitted a navy jumper to wear with mine and then one the same for Mabel. One day we were walking up the corridor at lunchtime and a chap asked us if we'd like to see the freezing chambers. When we went in, he shut the door and locked it. Our overalls went stiff, and we put our arms round one another and kept moving to keep our circulation going. At last the darn fool opened the door and did I tell him off. We might have stayed there all night and frozen to death.

Mabel had a bike so I bought one, too, and every Friday after work she'd ride home with me to spend the night at my place. She'd cook fish and chips for our tea while I did the washing. Then we might go to the pictures at the Torrensville Star; we sat in the front row of the dress circle, and if it was a spooky film Mabel grabbed me when it got scary and hung on to my arm when we walked home. If we had some people in for company and anyone made a noise when I sang my Irish and Scots songs, Mabel would tell them to be quiet. And often we sang duets; Mabel's voice had been trained and she sang from the throat. On very hot nights, we'd take turns to stand in the garden by the hibiscus bush and squirt each other with the hose – we didn't bother to put on bathers if it was dark, as nobody could see us in the back yard. Sometimes we'd get into our pyjamas and clear the floor and have a bit of a wrestle and see which one could get the other down first. We'd always end up laughing and going on silly, so that we had no power to fight with.

Mabel kept a pair of her pyjamas in the cupboard and slept in the double bed with me. We were very much the same sort of quiet sleepers, but I was up first in the morning and I'd give Mabel breakfast in bed. We'd sit about and talk and play with Mickey, or if we had any shopping to do we'd go to town and I might see some material and think I'd like a new dress. If it was hot we might go down to the beach and hire a little tent – Mabel had green knitted bathers, mine were maroon elastic, and Mabel copied me and got a white bathing-cap. When it was cooler, I'd make pasties and scones and put them in the wicker basket with the yellow and green plastic flasks, mugs, plates, knives and forks and we'd catch the train to the Hills for a picnic.

One Friday night after work, some of the Co-op girls went to a hotel to have a drink in the beer-garden for Christmas. I wasn't much of a drinker and asked for a shandy with a lot of lemonade. That one drink didn't upset my head but I sang all the way home on my bike. Mabel tried to shush me up and told me to ride on the inside because she was frightened I'd fall off in the traffic, but I kept my balance all the way. I even saw a two-shilling piece on the road and hopped off my bike to pick it up – who was going to pass up two bob? I was happy, that was all.

That Christmas, there were two tartan rugs in the drapery shop on the Beach Road, one red and the other green. Mabel liked the green rug, so I bought it for her Christmas present and she bought me the red one. We'd decided to go for a holiday together and thought it'd be nice to have rugs when we were travelling.

A notice was put up at the Co-op, telling us that a traveller in ladies' wear would be calling. He unpacked his boxes and hung garments on coat-hangers round the dining-room, so we could have a look at lunchtime. Mabel and I each bought a pair of grey mélange slacks; they were the first slacks we'd had and we thought they'd be nice to walk round in on our holiday.

Mabel had never been on a holiday before, and when her mother heard we were going she reckoned Mabel would be raped and her money stolen – her mother was a funny old stick. Her father was just the opposite, and told her to go while she had the chance.

I'd told Mabel she'd have to save her money for our holiday, so each pay-day she gave me as much as she could afford and I put the same amount away, too. I told her that when we came back and all our expenses were paid, we'd halve what was left.

We took our three weeks holiday in May (the best month to go, with sunny days and cool nights), and flew to Kangaroo Island for the first week. We'd never flown before and Mabel was scared, but as long as I was there she was all right and I kept talking to take her mind off it. We stayed at a hotel and I took charge of everything because Mabel didn't have a clue – she even copied what I had for breakfast. We both liked walking and beach air, and we had fresh scones for morning tea every day and went on the tour to the reserve. I always carried a packet of biscuits in my bag – when there were animals and birds round I liked to have something for them. The kangaroos came up and nibbled out of my hand and Mabel took my snapshot and we had after-noon tea under the trees.

We went to Victor Harbour for the next two weeks – I'd seen an advertisement in the paper for a flat to let, so we had our accommodation arranged. One night I had to borrow the lady in the next flat's husband to open our tomato sauce bottle. We did all the trips and I took over from the captain on steerage when we went on the boat trip. When we went to the trots I backed the winner in three races, though I wasn't a gambler.

[30]

Tom wasn't accepted for the War because of his eye-sight (it had never been the same since his fall from the roof at Holdens), so he kept working for the firm that installed sprinkler systems. He'd been with them so long that they gave him a leather jacket, leather gauntlet gloves and a matching leather cap to wear on his motorbike.

One night after the War, he came home from work to find that Louisa had left him. She'd taken Violet and the best bedroom suite and gone to live next door in her neighbour's spare room. She'd left Violet's bed for Tom to sleep in.

He had a nice house with a beautiful big garden but he didn't care a darn about anything after she left him, he just let it all go. He stayed there a while, then sold up and went to board on the Beach Road; but he took a dislike to his landlady and wanted to board with me. Twice I said no, but the third time he asked, I must have been soft in the head – I couldn't knock him back, he'd done me no harm and had always been a fairly good brother.

I knew what it was going to do to me, because I was enjoying my life; I knew I shouldn't have said yes. The girls from the Co-op came to tea a couple of times, but it didn't work. He'd come in and want to act the goat; we couldn't talk the same with him sitting there. It got on my pip. He talk-talk-talked and thought he was being the host. He had a deep strong voice and joined in the singing and just about drowned everyone else. It messed things up for me, so I didn't have the girls round any more.

Life wasn't the same. I had to get his breakfast in the morning and have his tea ready every night at six o'clock. Once he brought his friend, Des, home to tea and I heard Des say to Tom, 'I thought you said you had an old-maid sister.' And Tom said, 'Well, she is, she never got married.' I thought Tom had a darned cheek; I'd never have spoken about anyone in that way.

Tom did a lot of odd jobs round the house but he didn't like Mickey, he called him Old Flea-bag. We both had model mantel radios, the same colour and the same brand, but Tom's was a five valve and mine was a three. While Tom listened to his radio in bed at night, I'd be in my bed, listening to mine.

I didn't think I was very sexy, though I didn't know because I'd never had it (once you'd had it you might have been wakened up to it). The whole trouble was, Dad wasn't very sexy and it might have affected me in some way. Tom wasn't very sexy because he'd said he only had it once in three months (I'd thought I was worse than that – I hadn't had it at all).

One evening, at about twenty to six, when Tom's tea was in the oven, I thought I'd have time for a quick bath before he got home. I'd just dried myself and put on my brassieres, pants and dressing-gown, when there was a knock at the back door. It was Audrey's husband, but he said Audrey had left him. He came inside and tried to put his arm round me, and he followed me into the kitchen while I tended the stove. He kept pushing up against me and my dressing-gown fell open; I felt something against my leg and looked down and saw he had it out. I didn't jump, I looked the other way and said he'd better go. I had my eye on the clock, because it was five to six and my brother would be home to his tea, dot on the six, and if he saw Audrey's husband there'd be a fight – Tom would have picked him up and slung him out. Then I saw my brother go past the side window so I pushed Audrey's husband up the passage. He went out the front way while Tom went to the lavatory, washed his hands, then sat down at the table and waited for his tea.

I decided to rent some rooms to a woman and her husband, so Tom built a kitchen on the front verandah for them.

Hilda had already divorced a husband and she said to me that her new husband only had a little one (you could tell she was sexy because her mouth was always wet).

After my boarders had settled in, Mabel and I went for a fortnight's holiday to Melbourne. When I came home I found that Hilda had got rid of her second husband; she'd just packed his bag and put it outside and shut the front door and that was the end of it. She'd cottoned on to Tom and he was going up to her kitchen to have his meals. She'd helped herself to all my eggs – there wasn't an egg left in the fowl house when I came home from my holiday, so I put a chain round the fowl house door.

[31]

Mabel's boyfriend, Harold, had thin hair; he was one of the sort that went bald. He was a mama's boy, a bit sooky, and wasn't my type. Mabel had been going out with him for years; she was boss and told him that she didn't want to see him every night, and wouldn't marry him till she was ready.

Harold was one of the top decorators for Balfour's cakes and when it was my birthday he gave me a cream sponge iced in pale lavender and piped with ivory scrollwork, mauve pansies and my name. Mabel gave me a double-layer box of chocolates with mixed centres and one of the girls in the Butter Department gave me another box, exactly the same. I just ate and ate, I never stopped. I sat up in bed reading and eating chocolates, or knitting and eating chocolates – I didn't get sick but I went up to ten stone.

When Harold turned forty, Mabel thought she'd better set the date. He gave her a diamond ring and bought a block of land (someone else had got the corner block, but Harold got the next one) and had a new bungalow built with three bedrooms because he wanted children. I'd made Mabel's sister's wedding dress (she married a red-headed man and had eight children – red-headed men usually had a fair family) and it was altered for Mabel, but I made a new veil to go with it. I was at Mabel's mother's place from early morning to help decorate the tables for the wedding breakfast and then dress the bride. Harold decorated the horseshoe-shaped wedding cake with piped roses and feather plumes. It was just a quiet little wedding, they didn't make a big show.

Harold had to go to Kangaroo Island for Balfour's, so he used the trip for their honeymoon. I thought that Mabel would be lonely because those business honeymoons weren't so good, and she said she wished I'd come with them. But I couldn't push myself; though if she'd sent a wire I would've been on the first plane over. I needn't have stayed where they did, I could've stayed somewhere else. Or even if I did stay at the same place, it wouldn't have mattered because I'd have been in a different room. Mabel and I could have gone about all day; at night, when Harold came back, Mabel and he could have done what they wanted to do. I could have gone to bed and read a book quite easily.

Mabel left the Co-op to live in her new bungalow. She had gnomes with little red caps in the garden and green china frogs; there were autumn shades in the lounge and heart-shaped cushions in the best bedroom, but she couldn't get pregnant. She said to me that she didn't know what was wrong with her, things weren't right when they had the connection business, Harold reckoned he couldn't get in properly. I told her that if she really wanted a child, to put a pillow under her to lift her up (I don't know how I knew, I never had it myself). Once Mabel started with the pillow she had Kenneth, and then they must have used the pillow again because she had Bruce, and then after that there was no more pillow. Harold had got his sons and Mabel said that was enough.

[32]

I'd always been a bit delicate and didn't get my periods
every month; I'd only had a showing once in a blue
moon until I was about twenty-five. Then Mum had
sent me to the doctor, who gave me some pills to take
and I was regular after that, but it was a darn nuisance. I
wore white towelling sanitary towels and soaked them
in cold water till all the blood was gone, then I'd boil
them up on washday (I wouldn't throw them away,
those towellings). One day at the Co-op, when I was
fifty, I had a flooding and that was the end of it – I never
had any trouble when my periods stopped.

Bert was deaf, but he put it on a bit because Dot didn't
stop talking; she got on his nerves, so half the time he
made out he couldn't hear her. Bert and Dot had retired
from their farm on the West Coast and come to live next
door after the Lemons moved away. Bert was tall and
thin; Dot was short and fat, but she kept herself well
laced in. The garden was all higgledy-piggledy when
they came, but soon everything was put in order. Bert
cut the lawn and trimmed the edges every week, and in
the evenings he and Dot played bowls there while
people watched over the fence. Dot made borders for
the flower-beds from broken plates, pieces of china and
shells she collected. She wasn't much of a cook and
would dish up anything she could find for Bert's tea. If
I'd been Bert, I would have thrown it straight at her –

she'd just put a plateful of bones in front of him and expect him to make the best of it.

Bert did the gardening and Dot did the washing and ironing for Mr and Mrs de Dear, society people who lived up by the Cathedral in the flashest part of North Adelaide. Bert told me that Mrs de Dear was looking for a woman to do her sewing, so I went to see her and we got on quite well. I was sick of working at the Co-op (Mabel was married and a lot of the girls from the Butter Department had left), so I gave in my notice.

Mrs de Dear was a tall woman, even I had to look up to her. Mr de Dear was very short and had a habit of staring, but money marries money. He was well off and her people were well off – they had tons of money, Mr de Dear was a millionaire. Their house was a two-storey place with a lily pond and goldfish and everything you could think of – tiled bathrooms with fluffy rugs, a ballroom, a music room with a grand piano, carpets all through and a garage that held five cars.

When Mrs de Dear was out playing golf I'd sometimes look through her wardrobe – it was as long as the wall and full of the most expensive dresses, evening frocks and fur coats (if she'd caught me, I would have pretended I was looking for something to mend). When she couldn't fit any more clothes in the wardrobe, she'd have a clean out and give me a lot to take home. They were practically new, and I'd give them to different people in Pearl Street and say they were from the millionaires. I kept some beautiful nighties for myself, but you could see right through them.

Mr and Mrs de Dear wanted a son. They kept having children and, after five girls, at last they had Alasdair. She didn't have any more children, but once a nurse came when I thought she was pregnant – I think the nurse might have put it down the toilet and pulled the chain.

To begin with, I went in twice a week to sew, then one day Mrs de Dear had to go out unexpectedly and asked me if I'd look after Alasdair. He took to me, and from then on I was one of the family and went there nearly every day with Bert and Dot in their little green Austin. When Mrs de Dear went out she always told me where she was going and left the phone number because Mr de Dear was very fussy about Alasdair. He thought the world of me, that kid, and I made him extra pyjama pants as he was a bit weak in the bladder and wet his bed at night. If I went into the kitchen to have a cup of tea, Alasdair would sit on my lap and I thought Mrs de Dear got a little jealous.

If Mr and Mrs de Dear had an evening party, I'd be there to watch the children and Mrs de Dear would introduce me to all her friends. She never referred to me as a servant, I was there to supervise. When it was the eldest daughter's coming-out dance, the whole place was lit up – there were lights in the trees, a dance floor put down on top of the lawn, a big marquee, an orchestra to dance to and waiters in white coats for the drinks. But the eldest daughter fell in love with someone unsuitable and Mr and Mrs de Dear made her give him up; she went to her bedroom and howled for two days, so then they gave her a cream Holden car and sent her on a trip to England.

As I was working at the de Dears' so often, I thought I'd buy a motor-scooter. I answered all the questions right and got my driving licence and went to a shop on the Beach Road and bought a Lambretta in a light shade of putty. Lambrettas had just come out and I was one of the first to get one; the man in the shop showed me the gears and then I hopped on and rode it up and down the lane at the back. I paid him cash and then shot up the Beach Road and home. Tom's eyebrows nearly touched the top of his head when he saw me come in the gate. I took him for a ride the next morning and all the neighbours were out in the street watching; I went straight for a wire fence but just before I reached it my brain worked right, I braked and turned round and off we went.

I rode my scooter to work and put it into the garage beside the de Dears' five cars. Mr de Dear came down to have a look and sat on it to try out the seat. When Mrs de Dear had a big party I'd come home on my scooter to give my brother his tea, have my shower and off I'd go back again, all dressed up (I'd wear a nice dress but not an evening frock, because it would have been a bit awkward on the scooter).

When a Greek family came to live across the road, I taught the mother to speak English. Her little girl was only three and wanted to go out on the scooter, so I put a big cushion in the steel basket on the back for her to sit on, and I had a strap to hold her in. I made her a blue

dress and a coat and bonnet of velour so she'd keep nice
and warm. If I'd given her the clothes she would have
worn them all the time, so I kept them in my wardrobe.
She'd come over on a Sunday and I'd dress her; then,
after I'd put the roast in the oven, I'd get my scooter out
and take her down to the beach. We'd sit on the sand
and she'd just stare at the sea, as if she didn't know
whether to believe it or not.

[33]

After Tom and Hilda got their divorces they were
married in the Registry Office. Hilda had wanted me to
be a witness, but I wouldn't take it on – I didn't want to
have anything to do with them and their damn old
wedding. She'd already had two husbands and she'd
got rid of them both for no reason at all; she wasn't the
type to live peacefully with anyone and I didn't go much
on her for that. But I didn't show I didn't care for her. I
couldn't be nasty, it wasn't my nature, though I didn't
give them a wedding present. I didn't think they'd
make a good pair – Tom rolled his own and Hilda
smoked tailor-mades, he didn't drink and she did, he
didn't like meat and she was all for it, she was sexy and
he wasn't but I supposed that, like all men, he had his
urge now and again.

Tom moved up to Hilda's part of the house and I gave
them an extra room. As well as their rent, they paid for
their electric light. They used the front door to go in

and out, I used the back door and I had my garden, my cat and my fowls. Usually I kept away from Hilda and Tom because their marriage wasn't anything to do with me, but one Sunday I invited them down to my part of the house for dinner. I'd put myself out a bit and had all sorts of vegetables I thought would suit Tom. Hilda wasn't much of a cook, she only roasted and fried, and I could tell by his face that he really enjoyed it.

One Saturday I got on my scooter and went down the Bay to spend the day with Dorrie. When I got there I asked her if anything was wrong with her stomach – it was so big, and solid as a rock. She just slapped it and said it didn't worry her, but on the Sunday she collapsed in the yard. She went into hospital and they said it was cancer; they cut it away and she came home and seemed to get better. But you wouldn't have known it was Dorrie with all the weight she'd lost – she was back to what she'd been as a girl. Then one Saturday she came to see me and she'd fallen away to nothing. She'd gone so small and she had a black dress on that I'd made her, and it was hanging on her like a bag. She slipped it off and I ran it in for her on the sewing-machine and fixed it up so that it fitted.

Tom had an accident in his Humber Hawk car when he tried to pass a lorry. He swerved and the Humber rolled over, but he was still holding the steering-wheel when it came back on its wheels. The roof of the car was dented, that was all, so Tom drove on to work. But when he got there he felt funny and had to lean against a wall.

That night when I was in bed, Hilda came banging at my bedroom window and said Tom had taken ill. They had the phone on and she could have rung up the doctor – but no, she came and got me. Tom was stiff and grinding his teeth. It was horrible listening to him; he was grinding so hard I thought he'd break every tooth in his head, so I got a face towel and forced it between them. I told Hilda she'd better ring up a doctor, I had to tell her everything to do. She'd had three husbands but she didn't know what to do with them, except go to bed with them – that was the only thing she knew, if you ask me.

Tom went to hospital in an ambulance and they found he'd broken a blood vessel in the brain. The first day I went in to visit him, he looked all right but he told me the specialist had said it was a very ticklish job to operate on the brain, and he'd either end up in the asylum or in a wheelchair, or die. Tom asked me what I'd do and I didn't want to tell him because I thought Hilda might take offence, but in the end I said, 'I wouldn't want to end up in the asylum for one thing, and I wouldn't want to be a vegetable in a chair, for another, and the other one – it's death and you please yourself about that.'

The next day when I went to see Tom, his eyes were shut and his speech had left him and his face was all streaked with red, and a bluey-purple colour on the chin. Though he couldn't talk, he could hear everything that was going on and the nurse told me to hold his hand and ask him questions that he could answer by squeezing mine. One squeeze meant yes, two squeezes no. I was the only one Tom would recognize, he didn't even recognize Hilda and she couldn't understand it.

Tom decided not to have the operation and the doctors sent him home. Hilda went off to work just the same, so I took time off from the de Dears to look after him. He was mostly in bed, but sometimes he'd have a little bit of lunch with me; when he had a bath I'd tell him to leave the door ajar in case anything happened. Some men looked like monkeys with all the hair on them, but Tom never had a hair on his chest and he had pink flesh, just like a baby. I'd wipe his back for him and then he'd get into his underwear and I'd help him to dress after that. But then he grew worse and they took him to the hospital again.

I'd sit holding his hand and I'd be talking to him and he'd just squeeze my hand once or twice, he knew what to do. There was no pain but he couldn't speak, he couldn't move, he couldn't do anything. His face was all purply-red – his friend, Des, came to the hospital and fainted when he saw him.

Dorrie was in the Royal Adelaide Hospital, too; her cancer had spread and she'd been sent there a few weeks before Tom's accident. They were both on the ground floor so, after seeing Tom, I went out two glass doors and into her ward. One day when I'd just left Tom, the nurse came running after me to tell me he'd passed away.

Tom's workmates were given the day off to go to his funeral. They marched in front of the hearse and I'd never seen such a big funeral, with all those boys marching. Hilda had taken some pills to make her dopey and when we came home from the cemetery she passed out, so it was left to me to entertain her people. Still, I was used to entertaining.

Hilda didn't stay on at Pearl Street very long after Tom died. He was buried in September and she was gone by Christmas. She took everything of Tom's, and even the tools from the shed. Instead of giving me back the front door key, she threw it in the rubbish tin. But I was watching from the window and when she'd gone I got it out – she'd do anything to annoy me.

Dorrie died a month later, and after she was buried Vin said to take anything of hers I wanted. She was a different size to me so I didn't want her clothes, but I took all her knitting-needles. She hadn't been my real sister but it didn't make any difference – I'd always referred to her as my sister, Dorrie.

[34]

As a child, I'd often had pains in my wrists when it was cold – I was always holding them because they hurt. I'd had pains in my legs, too, and Dad used to rub them; he said they were growing pains and I took his word for it. As I'd grown older the pains gradually disappeared, but after Tom died they came on again.

The pains were mostly in my legs and feet and back. And my thumbs were very sore, too, and all puffed up. Dot would come in from next door and do up my bra in the morning because I couldn't get my arms round; and I couldn't bend so she laced my shoes up, as well – I said to do them tight or they'd fall off my feet. I sold my scooter because I couldn't use it any more, but then I couldn't even climb on to the tram (once there was a nurse behind me and she just put her hand under my bottom and up I went).

I couldn't even thread a needle to sew and I was dropping things – my hands were going so I had to leave the de Dears. Mrs de Dear said if I ever felt like coming back, she'd be very glad to have me.

I guessed it was arthritis before the doctor told me; he asked a lot of questions and put me on the invalid pension. Arthritis wasn't a nice thing to have when you were on your own; you'd got nobody and you didn't know what was going to happen or anything. I was fifty-six years old and sometimes I couldn't help thinking I might as well be dead. But then I'd think to myself that life was still sweet, even though the garden had gone wild and I'd had to get rid of the fowls and Mickey the cat had died (I found his fur in the paddock next door, months after he disappeared – I knew it was Mickey by the colour, grey with a creamy front, and his body was trodden flat).

The doctor gave me little tiny pills to take; I took them by the hundreds and after I left the de Dears I had four bad years that I mostly spent in bed. Everything I did was painful. I couldn't walk properly, but I got around – I had to. I couldn't do much cooking and I didn't want Dot to get my meals, because she had no more idea of cooking than flying in the air; but she often came in with a cup of tea, and Bert used to buy my bread. I always put my lunch cloth on the table at mealtimes, and my knife, fork and spoon. If I didn't, I couldn't sit down to eat. I didn't eat a great meal but I liked it right when I had it. But I never had a serviette because it wasn't necessary.

I shuffled along to the shops and if anyone was coming I'd stand against the fence to let them go by; I needed all the space I could get. It was frightening, I didn't know if I was going to fall over or not, and I couldn't bear anyone to grab me – when you're sore you can't stand it.

You can't hold a knitting-needle without your thumbs, so I couldn't knit. And I couldn't go out and get books so I'd read my Bible, I read it through about seven times.

There was nothing I could do about the arthritis, it was on me and I had to wait for it to go, or see what else would happen. I supposed that if I became really incapacitated I'd end up in a blooming wheelchair, hopefully an electric one so I could buzz round on my own.

For a while I was very depressed and then I'd lie there and think, what has to be, has to be. I prayed for help and that sort of thing (who else could help me? – it was in His hands). I began to think it was a period of time that was a judgement on me, to see whether I was really worthy of it.

It was in my feet and my legs and my back and my hands and one morning I couldn't get out of bed. After thinking it over, I wriggled to the edge of the mattress and let myself fall on the floor, so I'd have the bed to help me up.

I lay there about an hour before I could get up, and after that I always fell on the floor to get out of bed. I never bruised – not from that or any other fall. When I slipped over, I'd grab hold of a chair or the door or anything that would help me, even the gas stove. Bert and Dot said they didn't know how I didn't hurt myself falling. I said I had a special angel looking after me who let me down gently. It must have been true, because I fell such a lot of times and never got hurt.

What cured me I wouldn't know, but gradually I got better. I said my prayers, I took this and that, I had therapy – I'd lie on a table, face-down, while a woman massaged my back and legs; then a man came in and tried to pull my hips into place. Bert always drove me down to have my treatment and after a while he started having therapy (what for, I don't know) and then Dot thought she'd have a bit of therapy, too.

But my toes were still swollen and I couldn't wear shoes, so the doctor sent me to the hospital where they cut every toe open (I don't know why – to shift the bones round, I think). When I came out of hospital my feet were huge, and wrapped up in cottonwool and bandages. I made a pair of covers with elastic round the top that I slipped on so the bandages wouldn't wear out, and I made plastic covers to keep them dry in the wet weather. I didn't look to see if people were staring when I was in the street – I was dressed all right, except for my feet.

When the doctor took the bandages off, my toes were clenched, I couldn't straighten them. I had to walk on their tips and they got a hard skin on them that I filed off when it started to hurt. My feet were a darn sight worse than before I had the operation.

I thought it might help my legs if I rode my bike. When I started practising in the back yard there was no feeling in them at all – I just put them on the pedals and worked my knees. After a while I got a bit game and thought I'd try riding on the Beach Road. I fell off a few times but soon got the hang of it.

[35]

Dot decided to get baptized as a Jehovah's Witness, but she didn't have any bathers so I lent her mine. They were blue woollen ones and when she brought them back they were stretched out of shape (Dot had a big stomach). I'd liked those bathers but I couldn't wear them again.

I might have had arthritis but I'd never felt old, and when Dot wanted me to go to the Senior Citizens' Club with her, I said I had my own way of living and didn't want them. They were probably my own age, but they'd always seemed old people to me – I'd seen them wobbling round.

When television started in Adelaide, Bert and Dot bought a small set and used to ask me in at night to watch it. We watched *Hawaiian Eye*, *Cisco Kid*, *77 Sunset Strip*, *Pick-a-Box*, *Texas Ranger*. Prisks down the street had a bigger one, it was a His Master's Voice, so I got on the phone and rang up one of the big stores and asked if they could bring me down one the same. But they brought a Scharnberg Strauss by mistake and it was altogether different, it was clearer and everything was nicer – of course it was dearer, I paid cash. Sometimes the Warnes came in and watched it with me (they only had a wireless), but after a while I got sick of it and couldn't be bothered watching – I just turned it on every six months to see if it was still working and then turned it straight off. I didn't even bother with the wireless; I only listened to it for the time when the clock went mad. And I stopped buying the newspaper because it was only full of other people's troubles; if you'd known the people you might have sympathized or gone and helped them, but when you didn't I couldn't see any sense in reading about them.

Dot was always moaning that there was something wrong with her, and then one day she collapsed so Bert called an ambulance. I saw her fussing with the ribbons of her bed-jacket as they put her on the stretcher and took her away. At the hospital they found she had leukemia and before long she died.

Bert and Dot had been very close; one had never gone anywhere much without the other. Only four months after Dot's death they found Bert had cancer. His sister came to look after him and he seemed to fade away, without causing any trouble. He was never in bed; he just sat back in an easy-chair by the window, reading a book. One day his sister thought he looked funny and found he was dead.

And Mr Warne, the signalman, died and Mrs Warne had to go into a home. The Daleys died; the Turners died. Mr and Mrs Williams, who had the tennis-court, shifted away to live nearer to their married daughter. I'd liked Mrs Williams. She had a bit of hair round her mouth and was a woman who, if she took a fancy to you, showed her feelings – she always put her arm round me when we walked in the street, she brought me back a tea-towel from her holiday in Queensland.

The bottleoh sold the paddock next door and the Greeks built a church there. On Sundays incense drifted into my garden, bells rang, I could hear them singing but I didn't understand their lingo. Often they had a barbecue and a beer-up round the back after church.

The Church of Christ had Pastor Papa John, ex-president of the Hell Riders, and his Christian motorcycle team ambassadors to tell how Jesus changed their lives. The Coca-Cola factory had come to the Port Road, the Brewery gardens were floodlit at night; houses were ripped down and factories started going up everywhere. The Greeks built a supermarket where the grocery shop had been, offices were built on the tennis-court, and there were buses instead of trams on the Beach Road.

Planes started flying over Thebarton to get to the new airport. They came right over the house and, first off, the racket got on my nerves but then they seemed like old friends. I never pulled my blinds down at night and the lights of the planes shone into my bedroom – just for a few seconds, and the sound went right through the house. I'd count them in the night. Sometimes there were seven, sometimes five, and I knew when it was a big plane or a small one and whether they had a good load – I could tell by the engine.

A prostitute and her daughter came to live across the road; there were men coming and going all the time, she and her daughter were very busy people. Italians bought Bert and Dot's house and they reckoned they saw Dot's ghost; they described it to me and it sounded just like her.

I didn't feel old, but I was growing older in age, and everyone seemed to be dying and I thought perhaps I'd be next. So I went through the house and started to burn up old letters, photos, Dad's papers and things like that. Though the arthritis had left me, I thought it might come back again so I made myself a lot of clothes while I could sew. And I had the front garden cement-ed, except for a circle in the middle where I grew a privet bush; and I got rid of the hedge and the fern house and pulled down the grape-vine trellis, and then got the back fence done. The chap that did it brought his little boy with him; he was deaf and dumb, and I got on real well with him because I could speak deaf and dumb with my hands.

Plastic flowers came into fashion and I started buying them for the house. They saved a lot of bother and I bought roses, then daisies and daffodils, then orchids and ferns. Every month I gave them a squirt with the hose to get the dust off.

[36]

I hardly had a wrinkle on my face until I turned seventy (when I was sixty my skin was still like a teenager's), but my hair had gone white and I was deaf in one ear. The doctor sent me to a specialist who told me I'd have to go into hospital and have a hole drilled through the bone near the ear to let the sound in. He said he wouldn't give me a full anaesthetic because he wanted to talk to me while he was drilling to test my hearing, but he gave me an injection in my backside to deaden the pain. Doctors and nurses in masks stood round me on the operating table; I felt him cut beside the ear and flap the piece right back and then he started drilling into the bone with an electric drill. After he'd been drilling for a while he started talking and wanted to know if I could hear. It seemed I could, just a little, so I said he should do some more drilling. So he drilled on and talked in different tones and I seemed to be able to hear a lot more. But after the operation my hearing gradually got worse, though I never went stone deaf.

Then the arthritis, that I'd thought was gone for good, sneaked back on me . . . and it's as if something burning is going right through my hands; they're so sore I don't know what to do with them and I can't even straighten my fingers. They're always worst when a wind is blowing or when it's raining; then I always sit with them tucked under my arms to keep warm. When winter comes I never know what's going to happen, I just pray and often I'll have a little weep (about half a dozen drops) and then I'll think, oh, you silly old fowl. But sometimes, when the arthritis is very bad, I wish somebody would hit me on the head.

I don't think I'll be able to write to my friend in Melbourne, not until my hand gets better – I can write left-handed, but not much. If the arthritis hadn't come back I'd be on a boat or a plane; I'd be off.

It takes me a long time to get out of bed in the morning; when I wake up I can't open my fingers and I have to work my hands to get them going. And then I work my feet and wriggle them, and then when I've got right on the edge of the bed – it takes a good while – I swing my feet off and sit up at the same time; then I have to put my arm on the table to get myself up. And to get my pants on, I have to put them on the floor and wriggle my bad leg in, then I can pull them up and the other leg is all right. I put my bra round my waist and do it up, then turn it round and put my arms through. I can't wear shoes, so I wear slippers, and it takes me all my time to climb on the bus when I go to town. I try to be the first one at the bus stop so I can take as long as I want to climb on.

It's too much trouble to do my hair with my bad hands, so I go to the hairdresser in town. A young man shampoos it and I like the way he rubs my scalp, it's different altogether from a woman's touch. They always want to put a colour on, but I say no thank you; they have a great habit, when they take the rollers out, of teasing hair, though the hairdresser says they don't call it that now. I say I don't care what they call it, I don't want my hair teased because I can't get the comb through, and that's the end of it.

The doctor gave me some pills to take for the arthritis, tiny capsules with coloured stuff inside. They were made of plastic, but they were sharp, and I reckon that was what tore the flesh in my stomach. I didn't go to the lavatory for three weeks and then when I did go it was black. The first day I went twice and it was black, the next day I went four times and it was black, so I thought, well, something's been bleeding inside me. The doctor reckoned I had an ulcer and sent me to have an X-ray. You could see it on the X-ray all right, but I know it wasn't an ulcer, it was those plastic capsules that tore my stomach.

I'm one of those that take a long time to go to sleep; I have a too active brain and keep thinking of all sorts of things. Sometimes when I can't sleep I get up and make a cup of tea; other times I have a sing-song in bed. I sing party songs like 'Look for the Silver Lining', 'K-K-K-Katy' and 'The Sheik of Araby'.

In the wintertime the moss is just like a lawn, all pale green, right across the back of the yard and I have the fuchsia bush, the hibiscus, the agapanthus, the roses, and nasturtiums and button chrysanthemums. I can't keep up a big vegetable garden but when I buy a long-neck pumpkin I save the seeds and plant them, and last time I had eighteen come up. Sometimes when there aren't many bees round I'll pick the male flowers and do the inoculating myself, because I don't want to miss out on a pumpkin.

Sparrows and starlets, a couple of Murray magpies, and occasionally a few doves come into the yard. I talk to the birds, not in English but in whistle talk – the same sort of whistle as when they talk quietly to me. Four generations of sparrows have roosted in the Methodist church loft; I'll call them and they'll come down and get the food I leave for them on the moss. I always feed them at seven o'clock in the morning and they sit on the clothes-line and wait for me to open the door and come out with their bread or cake, or sometimes I'll boil up a lamb bone and give them that. I watch through the window and see them get their beaks right into it and there isn't a thing left on the bone, even the marrow is gone.

Once a sparrow fell into the yard and he couldn't fly, so I picked him up and felt his wing and it was dislocated, it wasn't broken. I pulled it back into joint and used a couple of ice-cream sticks for a splint and bandaged it up; then I lined out a strawberry box and placed him in that. I put it up the lemon tree and I'd dip my finger in water (they don't drink much water) and put it by his beak, and feed him a few crumbs of bread or a few seeds I'd picked out of the weeds or teeny little bits of meat. After about three days I decided to take the bandages and the splint off; I told him to fly, then walked away because they get a bit shy and timid. He fluttered his wings in the box and then flew up into next door's loquat tree. I wouldn't know if it was the same bird, but every time I watered the garden after that, a sparrow sat on the fence and wanted a bath with the hose. I'd turn the pressure down till it was just a fine sprinkle and he'd sit there and flutter himself round and round.

In summer, when I have short sleeves, the bees sit on my arm. They don't worry me at all, I think they love me; I just let them stay (if you brush them off they get cross), they're only sitting there to have a rest. The bees often come and sit beside me to die – such a lot do that and I dig a little hole, drop them in and cover them up, rather than let the ants eat them. When I pick off the dead flowers from the daisy bushes, I tell the bees they have to put up with me. But you must never talk loud to the bees, you must talk softly.